Secured Mail
KATE PEARCE

D1528182

ELLORA'S CAVE
ROMANTICA PUBLISHING

What the critics are saying…

ॐ

"Kate Pearce has done it again. What a wonderful world she has created in Valhalla. […] *Secured Mail* is a book you definitely don't want to miss!" ~ *Fallen Angels Reviews*

"I really enjoy this series with its strong Viking heroes and headstrong, determined heroines." ~ *Romance Junkies*

An Ellora's Cave Romantica Publication

www.ellorascave.com

Secured Mail

ISBN 9781419958694
ALL RIGHTS RESERVED.
Secured Mail Copyright © 2008 Kate Pearce
Edited by Briana St. James.
Cover art by Syneca.

This book printed in the U.S.A. by Jasmine–Jade Enterprises, LLC.

Electronic book Publication July 2008
Trade paperback Publication February 2009

SECURED MAIL

&

Dedication

𝕰𝕺

To the Hot Writer Babes and all the readers who wanted to know what happened to Sven.

Trademarks Acknowledgement

𝕰𝕺

The author acknowledges the trademarked status and trademark owners of the following wordmarks mentioned in this work of fiction:

NFL: National Football League

Oakland Raiders: The Oakland Raiders AO Football Inc.

San Francisco 49ers: San Francisco Forty Niners Ltd

Super Bowl: National Football League

Chapter One

ଚ

"Please don't kill me!"

Sven Magnusson scowled at the red-faced man he held by the throat, a foot off the ground. Yet another reporter who had risked his life scaling the eight-foot high walls that surrounded the Royal Valhalla residence in the Earth city of San Francisco.

"You are trespassing, scum."

He emphasized each word with a gradual tightening of his fingers around the man's neck. The reporter made a squeaking sound and his high color headed toward an interesting shade of purple.

"Magnusson, put him down."

Sven sighed as an all-too-familiar female voice spoke behind him.

"He is trespassing. He is endangering my king and queen."

"He's a reporter. The only thing he's likely to shoot is an out of focus picture of the queen picking daisies in the yard." She nudged his arm. "Put him down."

Sven clenched his teeth and gradually relaxed his grip. Ms. Cooper was right as usual. She insisted he called her that. Not Miss, not Ma'am or my lady, but Ms., whatever that meant. He couldn't risk killing a citizen of Earth. It would only result in the kind of publicity he was trying to avoid. With a grunt, he lowered the guy to the ground.

The reporter sagged against the wall, one hand struggling to unbutton his collar. "I'll sue, you bastard. "

Sven took a step forward and found his path blocked by Ms. Cooper. She placed a hand on his chest and tried to push him back. If he hadn't been so angry he might've laughed. She was six inches shorter than him and probably half his weight. One flex of his biceps and he could push past her and have her on her back within a second.

Her short nails, which were planted on his chest, were painted pink. Sven inhaled the scent of her perfume, some Earth flower he didn't know the name of, and imagined her flat on her back while he knelt between her thighs thrusting his cock into her warm, wet, willing…

"Magnusson?"

He stopped licking his lips and looked down into her suspicious gray eyes. Six weeks ago, Ms. Cooper had joined the elite squad guarding the Valhalla Embassy and Sven still hadn't gotten over it. Half the time he wanted to kiss her just to stop her telling him what to do. The other half, he just wanted to kiss her.

He rubbed his jaw and considered the angry little man in front of him. "He may leave quietly or I will call the police. Which do you think he would prefer?"

The reporter struggled to clear his throat as he directed his gaze at Ms. Cooper.

"I'll leave, but don't be surprised to hear from my lawyer." He pointed at Sven. "That guy is a fucking menace."

Before she could stop him again, Sven growled low in his throat and came around Ms. Cooper. "Get out, scum, or you will not have the ability to call anyone because I will have ripped out your vocal chords."

Sven smiled as the man headed off down the driveway toward the main security post. He would have to walk half a mile just to get back to the gate and his reception there wouldn't be pleasant. There was obviously another weak spot in the perimeter. Keeping the compound secure was as difficult as stopping sand running through his fingers. Sven glanced up at the leaden skies. If the man was really unlucky he'd also get caught in one of the San Francisco summer storms.

"Do you have to be so brutal?"

He turned to his companion who was regarding him with unfriendly eyes.

"If it means I keep my king and queen safe, then yes."

"But what happens if he calls a lawyer and sues you?"

Sven shrugged. "He would never live to testify."

Her lips tightened and Sven fought a smile. She was almost as easy to tease as his queen, Douglass, who also came from Earth. For some reason, Earth women didn't seem keen on men showing off their physical strength. Apparently, it was no longer considered civilized.

Sven continued to study Ms. Cooper. Her dark blue pants suit and gray turtleneck sweater covered her from the neck down to the top of her chunky black heeled boots. He had no idea what shape she was under all the layers of clothes she wore but it didn't stop him imagining. Despite the heels, she still only came up to his shoulder. Her skin was pale and slightly freckled. He smiled as a faint ray of sunlight escaped the gathering clouds and deepened the hint of gold in her brown hair.

"Magnusson, you're doing it again."

"What?"

"Staring at me in an unprofessional manner."

He dropped his gaze to her indignant face. "On my planet, appreciating a beautiful woman is not considered a crime. Why should I not look? I'm not touching you."

He took a step closer and she raised her chin to stare into his eyes. "Back off, buddy. I'm not beautiful and secondly, I'm at work."

He shrugged and started to walk back toward the palace. She hurried to catch up with him, her high heels crunching through the gravel.

11

"Hey, I'm still talking to you!" As he went to key in the door code, she grabbed his arm.

He stared pointedly at her hand on his arm. "But you make it impossible for me to answer you."

She frowned, wrinkling the delicate freckles on her nose. "What the hell does that mean?"

Sven sighed. "If I say you are wrong and that I think you are beautiful, you will immediately report me to your superiors for…" he clicked his fingers, "what is it you call it? Ah, yes, sexual harassment. My queen warned us that the ways of our Planet Valhalla will not always be acceptable here on Earth."

Her mouth opened and she shook her head. "I wouldn't do that."

He grinned. "Well then, I think you are beautiful."

She crossed her arms over her chest and looked down at the toe of her boot. "Okay, thank you."

Sven studied her closely. "Why is it so difficult for you to accept a compliment? Are all the men on this planet blind?"

"It's not that." She shrugged and tried a smile. "It's taken me a long time to be accepted by my male colleagues as just one of the guys. I'm always suspicious if anyone seems to be sucking up to me."

"I am sucking up to you?" Sven closed the outer door and reset the code. "In truth, my lady, there are parts of you I would love to suck."

Her smile disappeared and she stepped away from him as if he were diseased. "You are such a jerk. There you go again, making inappropriate remarks. What is it with you and the other Valhalla guys?"

Sven scowled at her. "You may say what you want about me, but I am proud of my planet and of my fellow bodyguards."

She met his glare head on. "You're right, I apologize." He went to speak but she held up her hand. "Not for saying you are a jerk, because you are one, but for including your friends."

He inclined his head. "I accept your apology on behalf of my companions, but I do not accept that I am a jerk. I have heard the queen use that expression to the king and I don't believe it is a compliment."

She started to walk away, her shoulder-length brown hair swaying as she turned to look back at him. ""You're right. It's not. Now if you have any more problems with reporters, come and talk to me before you get physical. I'm supposed to be the liaison between Valhalla security and Earth's Planetary Protection team."

He laughed. "And what would you have done in my place? Talked him back over the wall?"

She stopped walking. Sven braced himself as she stalked back toward him and poked him in the chest.

"*You* are a conceited ass. I'm fully trained in both martial arts and negotiating techniques. You know that. As the head of Valhalla security, you were one of the people who approved my integration into the security team."

He shrugged. "I simply agreed to my king and queen's proposal."

A flash of hurt in her eyes made him wish he could take the words back but she was already turning away.

"I will see you this evening at the security meeting."

Sven waited until she disappeared through the doorway into the main hall. He usually enjoyed sparring with her but today he felt that somehow he had erred. She'd seemed vulnerable and that made him feel unworthy. Did gaining the respect of her fellow officers mean that she had to deny everything that was female inside her? It seemed a hard way to live, denying who you were at your core. Perhaps he should talk to his queen and find out if all Earth women felt this way.

An alarm beeped on his wristband. He straightened with a smile and headed back up the stairs to the little prince's nursery. The king's apartment occupied the whole of the second floor. It was his turn to amuse the babe until he was fed.

Thea slammed all the doors on the way back to her office in the lower level of the security center. Sven Magnusson was the biggest asshole she had ever met. He seemed to think she was just some amusing little girl playing at having a job. She made herself some coffee and retrieved the day-old pastry she'd hidden in her desk drawer. Of course, like all the Earth team, she'd been briefed about the differences in Valhallan culture; their reverence for the few women on their planet who could bear children and their commitment to providing these women with sexual pleasure.

Most of the guys on the team had laughed their asses off at the thought of a society where women's sexual pleasure was paramount. Secretly, Thea liked the sound of it and had to remind herself that the Valhallan males only acted like that to make sure their women conceived. And that was not acceptable to any intelligent right-minded twenty-fifth century female.

She sat down at her desk and dipped the pastry in her coffee. Still, it didn't stop her wondering exactly how far the Valhallan males were prepared to go to give a woman pleasure. The three bodyguards, Sven, Harlan and Bron, who had arrived with King Marcus and Queen Douglass were outstanding specimens of manhood. All over six feet tall, endowed with toned, muscled bodies and faces as gorgeous as any current holo-movie star, they were certainly prime eye candy.

But, despite their reputation and their looks, she hadn't heard a peep about any of them having a fling with the female members of the staff. What did they do for sex? She licked a glob of frosting from her lower lip. It was a shame. In her dreams, one night with Sven would suit her down to the ground.

Coffee spewed out of her nose and she spat out a chunk of pastry. What was she thinking? Sven was *so* last century and after Mark, she'd made a decision never to get involved with a guy she worked with again. Her affair with him had not only broken her heart but almost wrecked her career as well.

She mopped up her desk and settled back in her chair. Not that she intended to get "involved" with Sven or anything. After Mark, she'd listened to her colleagues' advice and decided to play the sex game like a man. Love and leave 'em, especially if they start to get clingy. It had worked well for the past five years and she hadn't met anyone who'd made her change her mind.

She pictured Sven. Well over six feet of bulky muscular scathing magnificence. He would be a challenge all right. That auburn hair didn't go with an easy laid-back personality. If there really were so few women on his planet, perhaps he wouldn't be any good at sex? She shook her head. Nope, she reckoned he'd know just what to do with a woman. She remembered the heavy feel of his muscular chest under her hand, the steady thump of his heart. His feet were big too…

"Yo, Cooper!"

She opened her eyes to find her newly promoted boss, Matt Logan staring at her.

"Hi Matt, just daydreaming, what can I do for you?"

He smiled, displaying even, white teeth. He was in his late thirties, still unmarried and the closest thing to a best friend Thea had ever had. "Must have been a good dream, you looked like you were just about to come."

She felt herself blushing. "I was just thinking about what I was going to eat tonight."

"Yeah, right, more like *who* you were going to eat."

"Shut up, Matt and keep your mind out of the gutter. What did you want?"

He came through the door and perched on the corner of her desk. Reaching across, he snagged the last piece of her pastry and popped it in his mouth.

"I just wanted to talk to you about the meeting tonight. I hear that Sven Magnusson was beating the crap out of one of the journalists again today."

Thea sighed. It was impossible to keep anything secret in the small compound. As the new Valhallan public relations director on Earth, Matt needed to know when there was trouble.

"Yeah, Sven decided to remind one of the reporters from the *Inquirer* that he was trespassing on private property."

Matt frowned. "Did he hurt the guy?"

"Difficult to say. I don't think he broke anything but the guy threatened to sue."

"Of course he did, he's a reporter. We're going to have to talk to the king about this. Perhaps we could send Magnusson on some anger adjustment therapy courses or something."

Thea burst out laughing. "Oh my god, I'd love to see that. Please do it, please."

Matt looked puzzled. "Don't you like the guy?"

He's okay, I guess. If you like bossy, domineering giants." Thea sipped her coffee and hoped Matt didn't see the color still heating her cheeks. Sometimes he was way too observant for a man.

His expression sobered. "I need you to get along with him, Thea. He's our closest link to the king and I have to keep things sweet between us and the Valhallans. The clean up of their world is almost complete. Our government hopes that the king will be grateful enough to agree to take new settlers from some of our more overcrowded planets. In order to get the king to consider the idea, we need to treat him and his people well while they are here."

Thea stared at Matt. Despite their long friendship, it was unlike him to share intimate details of his complex job with her. Since his new promotion she sometimes felt out of step with him.

"Why are you telling me this?"

He shrugged. "Because you're a woman and we've noticed that all Valhallan men bend over backward to accommodate the needs of their females."

Thea put down her coffee. "So when you say, 'be nice' what exactly do you mean?"

Matt grinned and held out his hands palm up. "Not what you're thinking, so calm down. I'm not saying leap into bed with him. Just take the time to get to know him and get a sense of how the Valhallans will view a proposal on future immigration."

Thea stared back at him, a hollow feeling in her stomach. "I'm not prepared to get all chummy with Sven here. Its difficult enough being the only female on the security team as it is. In order to get to know him, I'd have to see him outside work."

"Is that a problem for you?"

"I'm not sure." She bit her lip. "Is this a direct order?"

Matt stood up. "Not yet, more of a favor."

"And if I refuse to help?"

He held her gaze, his blue eyes sympathetic. "You know what the Planetary Service is like, Thea, there's a record of everything and everything can affect your future." He leaned a shoulder against the door frame, a slight smile on his face. "Hey, perhaps at the meeting tonight, instead of anger counseling, I could suggest you as a possible mentor for Sven. You know, you could kind of help him learn to deal better with Earth ways—offer him the opportunity to hang out with you some more."

"You're kidding, right? If you say that, everyone is going to think I'm coming on to the guy! "

He winked. "Okay, I won't say that. I'll try to think of something else. I was only trying to cheer you up."

Thea scowled at him. "Then it isn't working."

"If you promise to think about what I said, I promise I won't say a thing tonight. And it would be better if the idea came from you. It would seem more genuine. "

"I'll think about it. Now go away. I've got to get my report done on the wall security breach."

As Matt's whistling faded down the corridor, Thea continued to stare at her cooling coffee. Her government wanted her to get close to a huge intergalactic Viking who thought she was beautiful. Did she want to get to know Sven? It was tempting. She considered her options. If she helped out, she'd only be obeying orders. No one would think she was interested in Sven for herself.

One part of her despaired that despite her efforts to blend in with the boys, they were only using her to get at the Valhallans because she was female. She threw the coffee cup in the trash. But perhaps it was the only way. The thought of one of the men trying to get close to the queen made her smile. The Valhallan males would probably kill him. So that left her, the only female bodyguard on the team, to save the day. She grinned. Perhaps that wasn't such a bad thing after all.

* * * * *

"My Queen, if I offered to suck up to you, would you be offended?"

Sven continued to rock the little prince in his arms as he watched Douglass Blood Axe, the Earth-born Queen of Valhalla complete her sit-ups. At four months old, despite his desperate need for a nap, the babe's intent golden gaze was fixed on Sven's face. Douglass groaned and sat up, pushing her long dark hair out of her flushed face. They were in the king and queen's bedroom which was dominated by a huge four-poster bed with black silk sheets and crimson quilts.

"What?"

"When I suggested that I would be very interested in sucking any part of her, she got mad at me."

"This person was female?"

Sven cooed at Prince Thor who obligingly gurgled back at him. "Yes she was. Why?"

"Because as I've told you before, you can't go 'round saying stuff like that."

"But she said it first!"

A stifled sound came from Harlan, his fellow bodyguard, who lounged on the bed behind the queen. He wore nothing but a thin silk loincloth and gold arm bands that emphasized the muscular strength of his upper arms. Sven tried to ignore him. Douglass wiped her face with a towel Harlan handed her and got to her feet. "What exactly did she say?"

Sven frowned as he tried to remember. "She said that she was suspicious of men who sucked up to her, or something like that."

"And you offered to suck any bit of her she wanted?" Douglass glared at him. "And you wonder why she was offended. She was offended, right?"

Sven gently held the baby over his shoulder and rubbed his back. "Yes she was, but then everything I say to Ms. Cooper seems to offend her."

"She's the female security liaison, isn't she? I haven't had much chance to talk to her yet but it's nice to have another woman around the place."

Baby Thor obligingly burped and Sven kissed the top of his downy head. "Yes and she seems to dislike me although I have no idea why."

Douglass snorted and reached for the baby. She tucked him back in his willow basket and headed for the bathroom door. "I need a bath. Will you and Harlan join me?"

Harlan picked up the basket and Sven followed along behind, trying not to frown. The bathroom was almost as enormous as the bedroom and contained not only a large shower but a deep bath set in the floor big enough for six. Thick cream carpet covered the floor and the windows were permanently shaded. The scent of roses hung in the steamy air as Harlan started to run the bath.

After checking to see if the baby was going to sleep, Sven stripped off his leather pants and white shirt and helped the queen remove her clothes. Douglass sighed as he rubbed her shoulders. He stroked the mass of bunched muscles at her neck.

"You are tense, My Queen. Are you missing Danny and the king?"

The queen dropped her head until her chin rested on her chest. "Danny is probably having a great time with his Granny at Disney Planet. He's probably forgotten I exist."

Sven laughed softly. "Seven year old boys are not known for their sensitivity. Would you rather he cried in his sleep missing you every night?"

"Of course not, it's good that he can get away. The last year or so hasn't been easy for him."

Sven silently agreed. Since his mother's marriage to King Marcus, Danny had exchanged his narrow life on Earth for the wonders of the Valhallan court and a stepfather who doted on him.

"I don't believe he regrets his mother's choice of husband."

"You're right about that. Marcus has been wonderful with him…"

"So if you are content about Danny, it must be the king you miss."

"He's been in Washington for four days now."

Sven kissed the top of her head. "And you have not benefited from his lovemaking. I will see if he is available on the live link. He will not be pleased if he returns to find you unhappy. "

He activated the link from his wristband and an image of the king reclining on his bed appeared on the bathroom wall. He looked tired. Sven bowed and gestured at Douglass who was about to step into the bath.

"Greetings, My King. Are you alone?"

"Greetings, Sven. Yes I am." He smiled as his gaze fastened on the queen. "Does my wife need pleasuring?"

"With your permission, Sire. Harlan and I would be honored to accommodate her."

The king nodded, his suddenly alert gaze fastened on his wife. "Will you let them touch you for me?"

Douglass smiled. "If you will watch and enjoy too."

The king undid his pants to display his already erect cock. He wrapped one hand around the base. "I always enjoy watching you come."

Sven picked the queen up and stepped down into the large bath, settling her on his lap.

Douglass relaxed back against his chest, the soft curves of her buttocks settled against his spread thighs, trapping his cock against her spine. His shaft hardened as she wiggled against him. He slid his hand down to cup her mound, making sure the king could see his every move.

"You should not wait so long to ask for our assistance. We are all still your servers. We are here to provide you with pleasure."

"I know that." She turned her head to look up at him. "You also remember that I said it was okay for you to go out with other women while we were on Earth don't you?"

Sven frowned. "Why would I want to do that when I can pleasure you?"

He slid two long, thick fingers through her slick warm folds until he penetrated her. Harlan entered the bath and immediately began to lick at Douglass' nipples. She shivered as Sven grazed her clit with his thumb.

"Because your vow to the king means you can't have real sex with me. "

The king's laughter boomed across the room. "Not unless you wish to die horribly."

Sven increased the glide of his fingers. "This isn't real?"

Douglass pinched his thigh. "You're being deliberately…ah…deliberately…oh, that's nice, don't stop."

He cupped her breast, offering it to Harlan's mouth. Harlan knelt up, his fingers working the queen's other nipple as he sucked, his erect cock grazing her hip. Sven felt her channel tighten and added two more fingers, knowing she needed to be filled well. He glanced up at the image of the king who watched them intently; his hand worked his shaft with strong, deft fingers.

"Touch Harlan's cock, my love. Pretend it's mine."

Harlan groaned as the queen reached out and took control of his cock, her fingers moved in time to Marcus' on the screen.

Sven rocked his hips, allowing his shaft to move in the constricted space between their two bodies. He loved touching the queen. He loved the scent of her arousal, the way her body tightened and gripped his fingers when she climaxed. He increased the tempo of his fingers, guiding her toward an orgasm as Harlan continued to suckle her breasts and kiss her.

The king groaned as the queen writhed in Sven's grasp and his face contorted with desire. "Make her come for me, Sven. I want to see her come."

Sven clamped his thumb down hard on the queen's clit and she climaxed, just as the king did. When she relaxed against him again, Sven came too. He closed his eyes and imagined he was inside Thea, her tight sheath fisting around his cock, his hot seed filling her. There was a disturbance on the screen as Bron, the queen's other server appeared and murmured to the king. The king groaned and rolled over onto his stomach.

"Once is never enough, My Queen. I look forward to pleasuring you in person in just a few days. Now I have to go and meet with the President's advisors and Bron has reminded me that I really need to shower." He blew a kiss at the queen. "I will speak to you later, my heart."

The screen blacked out and Sven lay back and savored the scent of sex mixed with the steamy perfume of the bath water.

After the death of his wife after only a year of marriage, he'd never thought he'd find another female who would allow him to touch her. The king's offer to make him one of his consort's pleasure servers had been an honor and a blessing he'd never expected. Pleasuring Douglass was a delight, although recently, when he was with the queen he'd started to fantasize about Thea instead. Sometimes it almost made him feel guilty because he'd come to respect and love the king's chosen one, especially after she'd provided the king with a son and the opportunity to restore their dying polluted planet.

"You should ask her out on a date."

The queen's voice shattered his sense of calm. "Who, My Queen?"

"That woman. Ms. Cooper. The one you want to suck."

Sven opened his eyes. "As I said, she doesn't like me. And what exactly is a date?"

Harlan nudged him, his long dark hair, shining with moisture, hung over one of his shoulders. "Haven't you been watching the entertainment system? The queen has been educating me about the shows called soaps about everyday people. A date is when a man or a woman asks a person out for a meal or to a holo-center."

"And what is the point of that?"

"To get to know someone."

Sven shifted his legs as the queen slid off his lap and turned to face him.

"Why?"

Douglass crossed her arms under her breasts and stared at him. "So that you can eventually have a relationship with someone that includes sex."

Sven imagined Ms. Cooper sitting on his cock, her breasts pressing into his face as she rode him hard. His shaft twitched.

"I do not need sex."

Douglass laughed. "Sven, you're a great big gorgeous man. Of course you need sex."

A stark memory of his wife's pale, dead face flickered in his mind. By Thor, he had no right to fantasize about any female. He got out of the bath, keeping his gaze on the bathroom door. Water slid down his body to pool at his feet. Grabbing a towel, he crushed it in his clenched fist.

"Sven?"

At the sound of the queen's worried voice, he drew in a guilty breath. "I am sorry, My Queen. The idea of betraying you with another woman seems wrong."

Warm fingers curled around his ankle. "I would not feel betrayed. I would be happy to see you find someone you can love for yourself."

Sven swallowed hard. "I thank you for that, but I still feel a little uneasy."

Harlan helped Douglass out of the bath. She came to stand in front of Sven, her soft face, full of concern as she reached up to stroke his cheek.

"It's not like Valhalla, here, Sven. There are more women than men on this planet. You don't have to fight to find one female and commit to her whether you get along or not. It's an opportunity for all of you to get to know women who haven't been sheltered and over-protected by their kinfolk. Women like me who can stand up for themselves and tell you whether they want to have a relationship with you or not."

"And if I made a child with one of them?"

Her gaze softened. "You don't even have to worry about that. There are many ways to avoid conceiving a child. I'm sure you'd be careful."

And if I wanted a child? Sven looked away and focused on the delicate features of the sleeping baby before the queen could see the question in his eyes. The idea of deliberately having sex without trying to conceive a child was a concept he struggled with.

He returned his gaze to the queen. "If it makes you happy, I will consider what you have said."

She stood on tiptoe to kiss his mouth. "It will make me happy." She turned to stare at Harlan. "And I'm including you in this, Harlan. I want you to consider dating women here as well. I'll tell Bron the same thing when he gets back with the king."

Harlan winked at Sven as he bent to pick up the baby's crib. "I'll definitely date a woman if Sven does it first."

Sven raised an eyebrow. "As if any woman would have you."

The queen slapped him lightly on the arm. "You don't have to make it into a competition. I want you all to be happy."

Sven rubbed the towel over his chest. If he asked Ms. Cooper out on a date and she said no, it would probably get the queen off his back for a while. He smiled at the thought of Ms. Cooper's face. He hoped she wouldn't slap him.

Chapter Two

೫

Thea smoothed a hand over her hair as the Valhalla bodyguards and their queen filed into the large meeting room. Harlan, who was dressed in his usual black leather pants and open-necked white shirt, preceded the queen. His hair was gathered at the nape of his neck apart from three narrow beaded braids at his temple. Despite his quiet, amiable expression, Thea found him much harder to read than Sven who tended to display his feelings more openly.

Sven came in last, scanning the people as he paused at the door. His large hand rested on the shoulder of the queen who stood in front of him. His gaze fell on Thea and she smiled at him. One of his eyebrows rose. She immediately felt foolish and converted the smile into a scowl.

Of course, he didn't know that she'd been told to act nice to him. He'd probably expected her to still be mad after their last encounter. He guided the queen to a seat on the opposite side of the table to Thea. Harlan took the seat to the queen's left and Sven stood behind her.

Matt cleared his throat. "Mr. Magnusson? Would you mind sitting down? It's hard to include you in the discussion when you're towering over everyone."

Sven frowned and then looked pained as the queen elbowed him in the stomach. He sat down with reluctant grace.

Matt smiled and took a sip of water. "Thanks for coming to this meeting. I realize that as the king is away, we might not make much progress, but I assumed you'd like to know how things are coming along on Valhalla."

The queen sat forward, her hands clasped together on the table. "I assume the king is being given this information as well?"

"Yes, of course. A transcript of this discussion will be sent to him in Washington. We would have included him on a live link but apparently he's in a meeting with the President."

Thea admired Matt's easy, relaxed manner. From all reports, the new Valhallan queen was no fool. It was hard to believe she'd only been a courier for the United Planetary Parcel Service before her ship crash-landed and she met King Marcus of Valhalla.

Sven cleared his throat. "The President is more important than the future of the king's own planet?"

Thea fought a smile at Sven's direct intervention. Before Matt could answer him, the queen said, "Sven, as the President is also the current chairperson of the Interplanetary Health Organization, and the man responsible for the plan to clean up Valhalla, then yes, he is more important." She smiled at Matt. "Please continue. I'm sure we're all anxious to hear the news from Valhalla."

Matt gestured at the white wall behind him. A series of images of Valhalla flashed up on the screen. "As you can see, it's looking great. The scientists say you and the remainder of your population should be able to move back for good in about two more Earth months."

The queen's face flushed with color. "That's wonderful news. It is such a beautiful place." She glanced around the table. "You must all come and visit us as soon as you can."

Thea smiled. She'd love to take the queen up on that promise. The idea of all those gorgeous Valhallan men in search of a good woman made her squirm in her seat. If they were all as good looking and hunky as the king and his bodyguards, women from Earth wouldn't need much persuading to go and settle there.

She glanced at Sven and found he was watching her. She licked her lips and slowly bit down on the bottom one. His pupils widened and his hand clenched into a fist. She brought her hand up to her throat as his gaze intensified.

"We would be delighted to send a team of observers back to Valhalla with you, Your Highness, in fact, we're counting on it." Matt said. "I'm sure the people of Earth would be fascinated by the discovery of this new world."

Sven snorted. "The idea is acceptable to me from a security standpoint as long as you don't bring any of your so-called media with you. "

Matt looked puzzled. "The press is an important element in spreading information throughout our galaxy."

"*Mis*-information, more like."

"We would take the greatest of care to screen any journalists who accompanied the team." Matt nodded at Thea. "In fact, I'll make sure that Ms. Cooper handles that part of the process and reports directly to you."

Sven continued to stare at Thea. "And I will get final approval on all the names submitted to me?"

Matt turned to Thea. "Ms. Cooper, can you answer that?"

"Mr. Magnusson, in light of your well-known contempt for the gentlemen of the press, how will I ever get you to agree to a single person coming along?"

The queen sighed. "Sven, what have you been doing?"

Thea tore her gaze away from Sven. "Mr. Magnusson had another unfortunate interaction with a reporter this morning."

"Did he hurt anyone?"

"Fortunately, I came along and persuaded him to put the guy down."

The queen's face lit up with amusement and a hint of approval. "You persuaded him? Good for you." She turned to Sven. "You should definitely liaise with Ms. Cooper. It sounds like she won't let you get away with anything."

"But, My Queen…"

Matt's smooth voice intervened. "Speaking of the press, I'd like to arrange a photo opportunity for the Valhallan court. It might be the best way to stop reporters trying to sneak over the wall. We can include some of the more reputable entertainment channels such as *Your Planet Home or Mine?* and *Greetings!* magazine."

The queen's blue eyes widened. "I'd get to be in *Greetings!* magazine? Oh wow."

Sven swiveled around in his seat. "My Queen, with all due respect, you will just be pandering to this planet's obsessive interest in our private lives."

The queen held his gaze. "But I agree with Matt. Isn't it better that we show them what we want them to see rather than letting them misinterpret what they do see?"

To Thea's surprise, Sven's mouth snapped shut. The queen waited a moment and then nodded. "I'll talk to the king. I'm sure we can agree to this." She smiled at Thea. "Please start compiling a list of possible attendees for both the promotional opportunity and the observation party who will travel back to Valhalla with us. Sven will be delighted to work with you on both of these projects."

Thea glanced at the tall bodyguard who was trying not to glower too openly at his queen. He was obviously as thrilled about working more closely with her as she was.

"I'll do that, Your Highness." She looked at Matt who was smiling benevolently. "If that's okay with you, boss?"

"That's perfect." Matt stood up. "I've streamed some more of the latest footage of the Valhalla clean up straight to your personal screen, Your Highness. Let me know if you have any questions after you've watched it."

"Thank you." The queen got to her feet as Harlan pulled out her chair. "I'll go and watch it before the baby wakes up." She placed her hand on Harlan's arm. "Sven, why don't you stay and work out a schedule with Ms. Cooper?"

Matt winked at Thea. "That's a great idea. Consider it a priority, Ms. Cooper. The sooner we get that list agreed, the sooner we can make arrangements for traveling back to Valhalla."

Thea remained in her seat as the others filed out leaving her alone with Sven. He continued to sit opposite her. His massive hands joined together on the table, his frowning gaze fixed on his fingers.

Thea took a long careful breath. She felt like she was at high school going through the agony of a blind date. But this time she couldn't walk away, she had a job to do. Matt and the team were relying on her.

"I'm hungry. Would you like to come out for a pizza so that we can discuss this further?"

Sven slowly raised his head until his brown eyes met her gray ones.

A pizza?"

"Yes, it's a very popular Italian dish made from bread dough, tomatoes and cheese."

"I know what a pizza is."

"Then what's the problem?"

He frowned. "Are you asking me out on a date?"

Thea leaned across the table until her face was an inch from his. "What the hell gave you that idea? I just thought it might be a more comfortable way for us to 'liaise' as Matt put it, while we got something to eat."

"Ah." He exhaled slowly, his breath stirring the ends of her hair. "I have offended you again."

She couldn't stop staring into his deep brown eyes which were edged by the thickest, longest eyelashes she had ever seen.

"You haven't offended me. I just want to make sure you understand that this is strictly business."

He smiled and her gaze lingered on his mouth. "I understand, my lady."

She retreated to her side of the table. "Right then, let's go. We can take one of the chauffeured cars, okay?"

"As I cannot drive your Earth vehicles very well yet that would be a good idea." He stood up and stretched. The muscles under his white shirt pulled the fabric taut over his wide chest.

Thea imagined those arms coiling around her, holding her so close she couldn't breathe. She licked her lips. "I can drive."

His mouth curved up at one corner and her warm feelings for him disappeared. She took a step toward him.

"I'm a very good driver."

He bowed, hiding his expression. "I'll meet you by the main entrance. I need to tell the queen where I'm going and get my coat."

Thea hurried back to her office to get her purse. She also took the opportunity to dash into the nearest bathroom and reapply her makeup. Just because it was a business dinner didn't mean that she had to look like an old hag.

By the time she reached the hallway, Sven was already waiting for her. He wore a long black leather coat and black sunglasses that made him look even more menacing than usual.

She pointed at his sunglasses. "It's nearly dark out there. Why do you need those?"

"My queen says they help to conceal my identity." He took them off and settled them on the top of his head. "Do they not please you?"

She stared at him. Didn't he know that he looked like dark sinful sex on a stick? "It doesn't matter if they please me or not. I just don't want you tripping over your feet and causing an accident when we're out."

He nodded slowly and turned to hold the door open for her. "I will only wear them if I see any reporters. Will that ease your fears?"

She walked past him into the breezy evening air. "I'm not worried about you. I'm worried that you'd bring me down with you."

He grinned. "Don't worry, my lady. I'd make sure I didn't crush you."

Thea persuaded the restaurant to give them a discreet table at the back of the room. Despite her caution, since they'd sat down, every single server in the place had managed to pass their table. It was Sven's fault. Dressed in black leather he was the finest eye candy she had ever seen. To his credit, he made no effort to acknowledge the constant stream of servers who offered him water, cocktails and dinner menus, his attention remained on her.

After considerable thought, Thea ordered two large pizzas, a salad and a side of garlic bread. She hoped that would be enough to satisfy her dinner companion who sat quietly sipping his beer. His long legs stretched so far out under the table, his booted foot nudged hers.

She propped her elbows on the red and white checked table top and smiled brightly at him.

"So tell me, where were you born?"

"On Valhalla."

She kept smiling. "Where exactly?"

"Why do you wish to know?"

Her smile slipped a little. "Because I'm making conversation. That's what we do here on Earth while we're waiting for our food to arrive."

He put down his beer. "I was born in a small village called Iron Fist."

"And how did you meet King Marcus?"

"I met him when I was selected to be one of his bodyguards."

"How old were you then?"

"Old enough to fight."

Thea sent up a prayer to the heavens for patience. "Old enough to miss your family?"

He looked away from her, his mouth set in a thin line. "Old enough to have seen them all die."

She closed her eyes for a moment. "I'm sorry. You're right. That's none of my business."

He shrugged and returned his gaze to hers. "It is a common enough tale on Valhalla. My family contained several females."

She stared at him. "Is that supposed to make sense to me?"

"On my planet, women are rare and highly prized. Other villages and tribes regularly raid their neighbors to secure females for themselves."

"That's terrible."

He shrugged. "That's life. The desire to procreate, to have a child is deeply embedded in most societies, yes?"

"I suppose it is, although most of the planets in our galaxy are trying to keep their populations down these days to preserve quality of life."

His expression was wry. "I believe the queen would call that ironic. We worship fertile women and other civilizations try to stop their females from breeding. My queen tells me that women on your planet are not always well treated by their men."

Thea paused as the server put the garlic bread on the table between them.

"Statistically, there are more women than men on this planet. Most of the men seem to think that gives them the right to mess around with a woman and then move onto the next one."

Sven picked up a piece of garlic bread and swallowed it whole.

"You sound bitter, Ms. Cooper."

She nibbled at the corner of her bread. "Please call me Thea, we're not at work now."

He took more bread. "But you said this was a business meeting."

She glared at him. "I know I did but that doesn't mean you can't call me by my first name. As long as you don't do it at work, I'm fine with it."

He nodded and his lips gleamed with garlic butter. She wanted to lean across the small space and lick them clean. "Then you must call me Sven."

"I suggest that we meet at five everyday and discuss the proposed members of the press team and the observation party. Will that work for you?"

"If it is all right with the king and queen, I will be there."

Thea sighed. "The queen probably has a good reason to believe all the men on Earth are bastards. She was left to bring up her first son alone, wasn't she?"

"She was." His expression grew savage. "I cannot understand how a man could abandon his woman and his child. If I had such an opportunity again I would give my life to protect them."

After his explanation as to the courting habits of the average Valhallan male, she had no problem believing he meant what he said.

"Women don't need men to bring up a child. We're perfectly capable of doing it ourselves."

Sven picked up the remaining two slices of garlic bread and held one out to her, one eyebrow raised. "Women are the givers of life. They are far stronger in some ways than men."

She waved the bread away, watching in fascination as he downed both slices and finished off his beer. Perhaps two pizzas wouldn't be enough after all.

She raised her glass. "I'm glad to hear you admit that women are the strongest sex. I didn't think you had it in you to be so honest."

"I didn't say that women are always the strongest." His considering gaze dropped to her chest. "I would be able to knock you to the ground in less time than it took you to say my name."

"I doubt it."

His brown eyes gleamed. "We will have to test out my theory one day in the gym."

She held out her hand. "You're on. I'll see you there tomorrow at five."

He shook her hand and kept hold of it. She shivered as he turned it over and dropped a kiss on her palm. The hot hard tip of his tongue branded her flesh. "I will look forward to it. I've often imagined you on your back."

Thea felt her skin heat and was grateful for the arrival of the pizzas.

Sven gave a murmur of appreciation as he bit into the first thick slice. "Some of your Earth food is strange but this pizza is good. The queen says we shall take the recipe home with us and instruct the palace cook on how to prepare it."

"Do you think it will be safe to go home again?"

He looked at her over his pizza. "What do you mean?"

"Well, if your people spend most of their time stealing women, will the queen be safe?"

"Since King Marcus took power, things have improved. He has encouraged tribes to negotiate with each other for women rather than just steal them."

"Don't the women have any say in this? You make them sound like cattle."

Sven winced. "Now you sound like the queen. She has great plans for the future of women on Valhalla."

"I'm glad to hear it."

"The king had already introduced laws to ensure women received the same education as men and access to the courts if they felt their families were forcing them to make a particular match."

"Good for him. I would've expected nothing less."

Sven snorted into his beer. The first pizza was gone and he was already halfway through the second.

"Don't you agree with the reforms?"

"Of course I do. There is nothing worse than a woman who is unhappy. Why would a man want to live like that?"

Thea found herself smiling back at him. Who would've guessed that behind that macho exterior lurked a man who understood that his life would be a lot easier if he kept his woman happy?

"Are you married?"

Sven's smile faded. "No." He drank more beer and then picked something off his slice of pizza. He held it out to Thea. "What is this?"

She squinted at the object and then sniffed. "It's an anchovy, why?"

To her astonishment, he started to blush. "An anchovy. That is good to know. Thank you for telling me."

"What about it?"

His gaze dropped to his plate. "Nothing, I just wondered what it was. The taste reminded me of…something else."

She squinted at the tiny fish. "What?"

He sighed. "This is a business meeting, yes? Then I cannot tell you or you will accuse me of getting personal." He sucked the anchovy into his mouth, his expression considering. "Mmm…"

Thea set her teeth. He was deliberately trying to wind her up. She should be used to being excluded from male jokes but this felt more personal.

"Sven?"

He smiled at her. "Yes, my lady?"

"If you don't tell me what you are getting at, I'm not going to order you any dessert and I'm going to tell the driver you've decided to walk home."

He stood up. "Perhaps I should start walking, then."

She grabbed his wrist and pulled him back down again.

"Fine, don't tell me. Be a jerk."

He winked at her as he settled back in his chair. "Do I still get dessert?"

Sven insisted that the driver take her home first. Thea sat beside him in the back of the maglev vehicle marveling that he could move after all the food he'd eaten. His feet were crossed in front of him and one of his arms lay along the back of the seat. Whenever the maglev turned a corner, his wrist brushed against her hair.

To her surprise, after the driver opened the door, Sven followed her out of the vehicle. She touched his arm.

"You don't have to walk me to the door, I'm a big girl."

He covered her hand with his own. "It is my pleasure."

She sighed and allowed him to follow her into the building and up the stairs to her second floor apartment. She paused at the door and turned to face him.

"Thanks for coming out to dinner with me. It was fun."

When she went to turn away, he touched her cheek.

"If this was a date and not a business meeting, would I be expected to kiss you goodnight?"

Her heart rate increased and her nipples hardened with anticipation. "If I let you, yes."

He took a step closer until she was pressed up against the door.

"And will you let me?"

In response, she lifted her head and closed her eyes. She heard his sharp intake of breath as he bent toward her. His kiss was as bold and thorough as she had expected. He tasted of beer and garlic and so male that she wanted to kiss him forever. Her body reacted instantly and she slid her hand into his thick auburn hair to bring him closer.

Soon close wasn't enough. As his mouth ravaged hers, she struggled to slide her hand beneath his coat to touch his back. He groaned into her mouth and picked her up until her mound met the hard demanding length of his cock. She couldn't help but rub herself against him, moving her hips in the rhythm of his thrusting tongue.

His hand clamped over her ass and held her still as he continued to kiss her until she wanted to rip off his coat and climb inside his skin. It had been so long since she'd felt so passionate about anything, let alone a man. With a moan, she wrenched her mouth away from his.

"Do you want to come inside? I…want you too."

He stared down at her, his mouth swollen from her kisses, his hard body pinning her to the wall. He closed his eyes as if he couldn't bear to look at her.

"I cannot."

Thea licked her lips and he groaned.

"Thea, I cannot. I would be…"

She pushed him away as a wave of embarrassment flooded her. She'd been on the verge of allowing him to fuck her in the corridor. So much for her reputation and her insistence that she only intended to be his friend. So much for her much repeated demands to be treated as one of the boys.

She manufactured a smile. "It's okay. I was out of line. I should never have kissed you in the first place, not that it wasn't fun, but as you said, this is strictly business."

He held out his hand. "Thea, you don't understand, that's not why I stopped."

She turned her back on him to key in the code to her apartment. Her hands were shaking so badly she almost couldn't manage it.

"Goodnight, Sven. See you in the morning."

She managed to shut the door in his concerned face and sank down to the ground. Oh god, she was so pathetic. She'd wanted him so badly. He'd been everything she'd imagined and more. The ache between her legs increased and she whimpered. She opened her zipper and slid her hand down inside her panties to cup her pussy. She was so wet, her fingers were instantly soaked. If she couldn't have Sven inside her, she'd have to do the best she could.

Sven cursed as he headed down the stairs to the waiting vehicle. Why had he turned her down? She'd been willing to take him into her bed and by Thor, he'd wanted to be there. What had stopped him?

He stared at the glass door in front of him as if the force of his frustration might smash it open it for him. He'd needed her to acknowledge that she wanted him and him alone. Once she was in his bed, she was his forever. That possessive instinct had almost overwhelmed him and he hadn't expected it. The queen had suggested he date an Earth woman not instantly decide to make her his mate. Perhaps the queen was right and he had done without sex for too long. Was Thea really so special to him or was he merely overreacting?

Constantly seeing the king making love with the queen had reawakened his old instincts to find and possess a woman of his own. Being allowed to touch and not have the queen had become difficult for him recently. He sensed that both the king and queen noticed it and were unsure how to deal with him. His smoothed a hand over his swollen cock. What he needed was a long cold shower and some privacy to relieve the ache in his balls.

"Mr. Magnusson?"

The driver was standing on the step below him holding a pair of blue gloves.

"I think Ms. Cooper left these in the car."

Blindly, Sven held out his hand and the driver dropped the leather gloves in his palm. He stared at them for a long moment.

The driver cleared his throat. "I'll wait if you want to take them up to her, sir."

Sven smiled at the man. "Thanks, I'll do that."

He slowly retraced his steps to the door of Thea's apartment. All was quiet. He leaned his forehead against the door and prayed to the gods. This was probably not a good idea. She was bound to be mad at him.

He knocked quietly; half-hoping she wouldn't answer. "Thea?"

To his amazement the door opened an inch. He held out the gloves.

"You left these in the vehicle."

"Oh." She sounded out of breath. He waited as she stuck her hand through the narrow gap. "Thank you."

He inhaled the sharp scent of her arousal and before he could think further he grabbed her wrist and brought her fingers to his lips. With a groan he carefully sucked each finger into his mouth and tasted her cream. His cock throbbed and hardened with each subtle taste of her desire.

"I have denied you release. I have denied you your woman's pleasure." He pushed at the door and it opened easily. Thea sat on the floor. His heated gaze fell to her pants which were unzipped and he groaned.

"Oh damn, you weren't supposed to see that." Thea's fingers fumbled with her zipper but Sven caught her other hand.

"I was right, anchovies do taste like a woman."

Before she could speak, he had her on her back, shoving down her already open pants. His large hand pressed over her silk-covered pussy and her thick cream soaked through her panties and pooled in his palm. He struggled to breathe.

"Let me do this for you. Let me give you pleasure."

Thea closed her eyes as Sven adjusted his hand and stroked her clit, his movements restricted by her silk panties. She looked down and saw how intently he gazed at her. With a sigh, she relaxed her legs as far as her pants would let her. He gave an approving murmur and drew the blue fabric down to her knees to give him more access to her wet panties and pussy.

"You are beautiful, my lady. I am honored that your body welcomes my touch."

His gently rubbing fingers made her want to lift her hips and ask for more. She arched her back trying to get him to slide his fingers deep inside her. With a growl he obliged, filling her with two thick fingers. Her pussy clenched hard around him and he groaned.

"Your channel is tight and yet you welcome me." Thea bit her lip as he kept his fingers still and deep. He studied her flushed face, his eyes full of lust.

"If you allow me to pull your panties down, I will be able to service you better."

She nodded, trembling, as his hand slid over her buttocks pulling the scrap of silk away, exposing her to his gaze. His fingers remained embedded inside her and his thumb toyed with her clit bringing her closer to a climax. She reached down and grabbed his thick wrist.

"Please."

He crouched over her and kissed her mouth. "If that is your wish, my lady."

He began to move his fingers, widening them within her, withdrawing at the end of almost every hard stroke, the palm of his hand slamming into her sex. Thea concentrated on the slick wet sound of his fingers, the slap of his flesh against hers. He moved lower and she almost screamed when his mouth joined the torment, licking and sucking at her clit until she came with a violence that made her shake and dig her nails into his shoulder. How had he known that she fantasized about sex just like this? Hard and fast, taking everything she had to give without offering her a chance to resist.

He continued to lick at her as she recovered her senses, the brush of his unshaven cheek a continuous burn against her lax inner thighs. He knelt back and stared at her.

"Thank you, my lady. Let me help you to bed."

Before she could answer him, he swept her up in his arms and headed toward the back of her apartment. The door of her bedroom was open and he carefully laid her down on the bed. From her position she could clearly see his enormous erection straining the front of his leather pants.

She reached out to touch him and he shivered.

"Sven, you don't have to go, stay with me, please."

He smiled down at her, his expression regretful. "I have to go. With Bron away, I must share night time duties with Harlan to protect the queen and prince."

Thea rolled onto her side and grabbed hold of the sheet, pleating it between her fingers.

"That's just an excuse. You don't want to stay, do you?"

He knelt by the side of the bed and took her hand. "My lady, if I stay with you, I will never let you go, is that what you want?"

She stared into his intent eyes. God, he was serious. That was the last thing she wanted to discuss right now. She sighed.

"Perhaps it's better if you leave. We can talk about this mess in the morning."

Was that a flash of disappointment in his eyes? Before she could ask, he lowered his head and kissed her slowly on the mouth. She tasted the scent of her own arousal and imagined his big muscled body moving over hers, his cock filling her pussy. It took all her resolve to end the kiss and release him.

"Goodnight, Sven."

"Goodnight, my lady."

She waited until she heard the front door close behind him before rolling over onto her stomach. In five minutes, Sven had given her the best sexual experience of her life. What would he be like for a whole night? She shivered at the delicious thought. It was definitely time to follow her own advice, get out of her clothes, have a shower and stop thinking about what might have been until the morning.

Chapter Three

❧

"So, how was it, then?"

Thea sat up so quickly that she almost fell off her office chair.

"It wasn't, we didn't do anything. It was…oh crap."

Thea tried to stare Matt down as his evil grin appeared.

"Methinks the lady protests too much. What exactly didn't you do?"

She struggled to gather her thoughts. "Sven and I had a nice dinner together and agreed to meet up at the end of each day and work on the list for the away team and the accompanying press."

He winked as he settled on the edge of her desk. "So its *Sven* now, is it?"

Thea raised an eyebrow. "You're the one who asked me to get to know him."

"So how was he?"

"In what way?"

"In any way."

"It depends. Are you asking me this as a friend or as my boss?"

Matt's smile deepened. "As your friend, of course, spill."

Thea sat back in her chair. "He was surprisingly nice. Despite the fact that every woman in the place, and a few of the guys, tried to flirt with him, he kept his attention on me. It was quite refreshing."

"Well, Valhallan men are supposed to be attentive to their women. Remember, they can't afford to lose them too easily."

"Not like the guys on Earth then who think its okay to hit and run."

"And it's not just the guys."

Thea frowned. "What's that supposed to mean?"

"You're not exactly renowned for your ability to stick around either."

She fixed him with an accusatory stare. "I learned from a master—you."

Matt retreated toward the door. "I didn't expect you to take my lessons quite so much to heart. You haven't had a proper relationship for five years."

"And you have?"

He sighed. "At least I'm looking. You never give a guy a chance."

"That's not fair, Matt. Since Mark humiliated me so publicly, it's been hard to trust anyone again."

"I know that, sweetheart, but you're twenty-eight now and Mark's been married for four years. Don't you think it's time you gave yourself a break?"

A familiar burning sensation rolled around in her stomach. "So what are you saying? I should get it on with Sven? That would work out great for you wouldn't it?"

He paused in the doorway, one hand braced on the frame. "What's that supposed to mean?"

"I get close to Sven and you get kudos from the higher-ups."

All traces of humor disappeared from his face. "You really think I'd use you like that?"

She shrugged. "Why not?"

He grabbed the door handle. "Sometimes, Thea, you are such a bitch."

She winced as he slammed the door behind him. With a groan, she buried her head in her hands. Why had she reacted so defensively? Matt hadn't really told her anything she hadn't worked out painfully for herself. So she liked rejecting men before they rejected her first. What was wrong with that? It was all Sven's fault for muddling her senses last night. Everything had seemed perfectly clear right up until she'd let him lick and suck her to a climax.

She wiggled in her seat as memories of his head between her thighs surfaced to taunt her. How was she going to face him today? She closed her eyes and kept her head down. Perhaps by the end of the day she would've have figured out how to apologize to both men.

"So how was it then?"

Sven scowled at Harlan who sat behind him in the queen's bathroom. He continued to shave, his attention on the dangerous curve of his chin and the sharpness of his blade.

"It was none of your business."

Harlan grinned. "Sven, you spent half an Earth hour in the shower when you came back from dining with Ms. Cooper. Either you were cleaning off her scent or relieving your frustrations." His deft fingers returned to braiding the black hair at his temple. "From the sour look on your face, I assume it was the latter."

Sven glanced at the queen's bedroom door which remained closed. He put down his shaving blade.

"Last night I was sorely tempted to lie with another woman."

Harlan followed his gaze. "But the queen said it was acceptable for you to do that."

Sven shrugged. "She suggested I get a date. Not leap into bed with the first woman I go out with. And I gave my vow to the queen *and* the king. How do I tell the king that I have found a woman more desirable than his wife?"

"The king will understand."

"The king is within his rights to kill me." Sven lowered his voice. "But what if I wish to keep my vows as well? I am fond of the queen."

"We all are." Harlan finished the first thin braid and started on the second. "In truth, the king offered you a position as his consort's server, not his queen's. And I don't know if you've noticed, but he doesn't seem to need much help from us to satisfy her. In fact, he doesn't need us at all when he is here." He glanced up at Sven. "Don't you want your own woman?"

Sven splashed water on his face and grimaced as he slapped on some aftershave. "It's been many years since I've lived with a female, I'm not sure."

Harlan sighed. "I would like a wife. Seeing the king so happy with the queen makes me yearn for things I have never had."

"Then go out and find someone. You have permission."

Harlan finished his braiding and sat cross-legged on the carpet. "I'm waiting for her to find me."

"You seem very certain."

"I am. She is close now. She will be here soon. All I have to do is wait." Harlan's serene conviction made Sven uneasy. His friend had an uncanny ability to read the future. Harlan continued to talk, his thoughtful gaze fixed on Sven.

"It might be possible for you to gain release from your vows." He smiled at Sven's unconvinced expression. "We would have to ask Thorlan to consult the law and see what the proper procedure is." He stood up. "This woman. Is she worth losing your position of trust with the king?"

Sven threw his towel to the ground and strode to the window, his back to Harlan. "All I know is that when I'm with her, I want to possess her, not date her as the queen suggested."

"Despite your doubts you wish to make her your wife?"

"How can I feel like this when I've only known her for a few weeks? Perhaps the queen is right and I am so desperate to have sex again that I've gone mad for the first woman I've seen."

"Ms. Cooper is hardly the first woman you've seen. There are hundreds of available females here on Earth."

Sven turned to stare at his friend with dawning respect. "That is true and she is the only one who interests me."

Before he could continue, the door to the queen's bedroom opened and Douglass emerged carrying her son in her arms. Sven hurried across to take the boy, wrinkling his nose at the sour smell.

"I'll change him for you, My Queen. Harlan, attend the queen's bath."

Harlan bowed to the queen, his smile as tranquil as ever. Sven tensed as the outer door to the Royal suite burst open to reveal a smiling King Marcus and Bron.

"Marcus, you are back early!"

The queen squealed and ran straight into the king's arms, which locked around her. Oblivious to the other men, he picked her up and kissed her with an intensity that demanded privacy.

Eventually, the king caught Sven's gaze. "Can you take care of my son for a little while?"

Sven winked at the baby as his parent's disappeared into the bedroom without a backward glance. "You'll get used to them doing that. After five days apart, the king is probably desperate to spill his seed."

Bron laughed. His blond hair gleamed in the light as he ran his fingers through it. He was the youngest of the queen's three servers. He looked as if he'd just woken up from a refreshing nap rather than spent the day traveling with an irritable king.

"Aye, that's the truth. He's been a bear for the last two days. I was glad to return." He hugged Harlan and came across to smile down at the babe. He wrinkled his nose at the smell.

"How is our young prince? Still keeping everyone awake at night?"

Sven snorted. "You've only been gone a few days, nothing has changed."

Harlan cleared his throat. "Apart from the fact that Sven has found himself a woman."

Bron stopped smiling at the baby to stare at Sven.

"You have a woman?"

"I do not. Harlan is trying to be amusing and failing as usual."

Bron continued to stare at him. "And what does the queen think about that? You have always been her favorite."

Abruptly, Sven passed the baby to Bron. "I have to attend a security meeting about the perimeter wall. You and Harlan will have to look after the young prince." He glanced at the bedroom door. "I doubt the king will let the queen out of bed for a long while. Be prepared to call the nanny woman if the baby needs anything."

Harlan's soft laugh stopped him at the door. "Are you running away from us, Sven or are you so enamored of Ms. Cooper that you can't bear to be from her side?

Sven clenched his fists. "I am going to meet with Mr. Matt Logan to discuss increasing the security patrols around the wall." He held Harlan's gaze. "Is there anything else you want to say to me?"

Harlan closed his mouth and shook his head. Bron followed suit.

"Good, then I will see you both later. Let me know when the king emerges. I need to speak to him."

He resisted the temptation to slam the door and moved swiftly down the corridor. His steps slowed when he reached the main hallway. He did have a meeting with Matt Logan but it wasn't for another half an hour. Should he seek out Ms. Cooper and try to make things right with her?

His feet took him out of the house and into the extensive gardens behind the property. Fingers of white fog drifted over the high wall, wrapping themselves around the treetops and diluting the weak power of the sun. Sven shivered in his thin cotton shirt. He missed Valhalla's hot dry air, the shimmering purple desert sand and the two suns. The San Francisco fog, which moved with a speed that surprised him, was not to his taste at all.

If he found Ms. Cooper he would probably just make things worse. He wasn't used to sharing his feelings with anyone, let alone a woman. The queen insisted it was important but he had yet to be convinced. Showing an enemy that you were vulnerable could never be a good thing.

He spotted a secluded stone bench under an arch covered with fragrant yellow flowers and headed for it. Intellectually, he knew women weren't the enemy but he had protected his heart for many years and somehow they had come to seem like that. He buried his head in his hands. The sweet scent of the early blooming flowers reminded him of the lushness of a Valhalla evening, the welcoming scent of a woman's body. Ms. Cooper deserved to be loved and cherished as did all women. What chance would a man like him have with her anyway? He wasn't even sure if he was capable of sustaining a loving relationship.

The trouble was, he wanted her badly. Just thinking of the taste of her sex made him hard again. He sat back and absently rubbed his palm over his erect shaft, enjoying the caress of his leather pants and zipper on his rapidly hardening flesh. Would Ms. Cooper like his cock? She'd seemed impressed when she'd touched him last night.

Sven groaned and cast a quick glance around him. The garden was deserted and he knew that none of the security cameras were aimed at this part of the property. He couldn't go to his meeting with a hard-on. With more haste than grace, he unzipped his pants, grunting as the metal teeth grazed his skin. He closed his fist around the base of his shaft and pumped hard. Pre-cum soon made his movements easier as it coated his working fingers. He imagined Thea Cooper's mouth closing around his cock, her teeth nibbling at his heated flesh.

He'd been rough with her last night and she'd taken everything without complaint. With a moan, he flexed his shoulders where the small burn from her embedded fingernails still lingered. What would she do to him in the throes of her pleasure when his cock was buried deep inside her? Draw blood, he imagined, mark him permanently as her own, let him bite and take in return.

From the corner of his eye, he caught a flash of movement in one of the second-floor windows in the security center. Thea's startled face appeared briefly and then disappeared. Sven smiled. Sometimes the gods were kind. He hadn't anticipated an audience but he was more than willing to perform. He angled his body toward the window and started to move his fingers again. Slower this time, showing her the full extent of his cock and how aroused he was. Would she stay and enjoy the show? He hoped it excited her as much as it did him.

He cupped his balls in his left palm and wrapped his fingers around his shaft. With his right hand, he played roughly with the crown of his cock, enjoying the pleasure that bordered on pain, turned on by the thought of Thea watching him touch himself. Would she be wet for him now? Her panties soaked with cream, her clit swelling and begging for his mouth?

By Thor, he wanted to go to her office, spread her legs wide and shove himself inside her in one strong mighty thrust. He knew she'd take him like that. Hard and fast without mercy. Her body so wet for him that he'd slide inside and fill her until she climaxed again and again. He started to pant and stare up at her window, willing her to see his desire, to know that he wanted her as much as she wanted him.

Oh. My. God.

Thea took another surreptitious peep out of the hall window. She hadn't been mistaken. It was Sven sitting in the garden. And he wasn't just sitting. He was...playing with himself. She licked her lips as her panties were swamped with moisture. His cock was everything she had imagined. Wide enough to make her wonder if he'd fit and long enough to make her desperate for a chance to try him on for size. Did he know she could see him? Did he realize that other people might be able to see him as well?

His fist moved fast, his movements rough as he worked his swollen cock. He kept his attention on her window, as if he wanted her to see all of him, to know that all she had to do was ask and that raw rough masculinity could be hers. She felt her face heat up and her body react. If he came to her now, she'd let him take her on her desk, she knew it.

A sound behind her made her jump. Dammit, she was at work! She couldn't behave like this in front of her colleagues. She'd made a fool of herself with Mark and she couldn't make that mistake again. She forced herself to pause and consider the consequences. If someone complained, Sven could face charges of indecent exposure. Rather than yelling out of the window and attracting attention, perhaps it would be best if she went down and told him to cover himself up. She grabbed her jacket and headed for the stairs.

His wristband beeped a five minute warning and Sven increased the tempo of his fingers. He had to finish now and get to the meeting with Matt. Seeing Thea, the object of his fantasies, had raised his level of excitement beyond his ability to simply stop. He groaned as his cum spurted through his fingers and searched for a handkerchief in his pocket. Not much time to set himself to rights and get to the meeting room. He grimaced as the tender flesh of his shaft rubbed against the now wet leather.

When he reached the meeting room, he paused to smooth down his hair and check he was presentable. With a calm smile, he opened the door and found Matt already waiting for him.

"Morning, Magnusson. How's it hanging?"

Sven immediately fought an urge to clutch at his groin. Was something amiss?

He nodded. "It is hanging well, thank you. How is yours hanging?"

Matt grinned. "None of your business."

Sven tried not to let his confusion show as he took a chair and sat at the table. He frowned at Matt. "Did I misspeak?"

"Not really. It's my fault actually. I forget you don't use the same expressions on Valhalla as we do on Earth."

"Ah, so when you asked me how 'it' was hanging, it was a rhetorical question."

"Well, I just meant how you were doing. These days, that qualifies as a rhetorical question. Nobody really want to know, right?"

"Why not?" Sven rested his hands on the table in front of him. He still wasn't sure if he trusted Matt Logan. The man smiled too much and seemed much too close to Thea. "Why don't your citizens care about each other?"

"I reckon it's because our planet has gotten so crowded that we all resent anyone who invades our personal space. And getting to know someone means you allow them into your space and then you have to care about them."

"But it is good to care about people."

Matt smiled. "I'm not disagreeing with you, Sven, but it can be hard sometimes." He sat down across the table. "Take Ms. Cooper for example. She hasn't dated a guy in five years."

Sven crossed his arms and tipped his chair back. "Perhaps she is too busy."

"Perhaps she just hasn't found a guy brave enough to invade her personal space."

Sven studied Matt. He had heard rumors that Thea and Matt were close friends.

"She is a fine woman and would make any man a formidable mate."

Matt winked. "Well, I haven't thought about her in terms of mating before but I can definitely see what you are getting at. She needs a strong guy to match her strength."

"A man like me?" Sven held Matt's gaze. "Are you a member of her tribe or family?"

"I'm not sure I understand you."

"It seems as if you are offering her to me."

Matt held up his hands. "Hey, I'm not doing that. What do you think I am, her pimp?"

Sven frowned. "Now I do not understand you at all."

Matt sighed. "How about we start this conversation over? It's getting way too complicated. Let's just stick to the security issues, okay?"

The door burst open and Thea fell in. Her distracted gaze flew straight to Sven. She was breathing hard, her color high. Sven stood up. He could see her tight nipples through the thin fabric of her blouse.

"Is there something wrong, my lady?"

She flapped a hand at him as she struggled to catch her breath. "Don't call me that. I saw you…in the garden…I went to find you."

Sven gave a slow satisfied smile. "You saw me? Did I please you?"

Thea's gaze shifted to Matt who was watching them with extreme interest. "No! I just thought you should know you were going to be late for your meeting."

"But I was *coming*. You must have realized that."

Sven fought a smile as she straightened and glared at him. "You are a jerk."

He bowed. "I aim to please, my lady."

"Don't call me that!"

Matt cleared his throat. "I have no idea what's going on here, but are you staying, Thea? If so, pull up a chair, otherwise get out."

Thea said something over her breath, turned around and shut the door with an audible click behind her.

Matt studied Sven. "Well, it seems we are both in the doghouse now."

"The doghouse?"

Matt groaned. "Let me explain…"

Chapter Four

&

It was five o'clock and there was no sign of Sven. Restlessly, Thea got up and headed for the door of her office. Perhaps it was better if she didn't see him this evening. She was still far too aware of his magnificent body, the size of his cock and what she'd like him to do to her.

If he couldn't be bothered to leave her a message she would simply assume he wasn't interested in liaising with her anymore. Possibly having sampled her charms, he'd decided she wasn't worth his attention. Her stomach knotted. It served her right for turning him down. If she'd let him stay last night all her worries would've been over by today.

In her agitation, she headed up the stairs to the large gymnasium on the ground floor. Why should she even care what Sven thought? It wasn't as if they were dating or anything. She stared at the door to the women's changing room. Lifting weights and thumping a few machines around suddenly seemed like a great idea. She opened the door and inhaled the steamy scent of the showers, deodorant and sweaty bodies. Inside her locker, she was glad to find a clean set of workout gear. She slid into the one piece pink leotard and laced her shoes.

At this hour, the gym was almost deserted. Thea was delighted. With the mood she was in, she doubted anyone would find her good company. She started with stretches, having learned the painful lesson of launching into something too quickly several years before. After Mark walked out on her, she'd used the gym to channel her anger and emotions into something positive and it was a habit she'd kept up. Although her main job was to liaise these days, she was as fit as the male bodyguards.

She eyed the first machine and pictured Sven's face. Yeah, that felt good. She soon found a regular rhythm, her arms pumping hard, her breathing steady. She only realized that someone had entered the room because of the swirl of cold air over her shoulders. She didn't bother to glance up. Most of the other guys knew her well enough not to try to distract her when she was working out.

As she worked her triceps and biceps, the machine counted down the seconds. She pushed through the fatigue, allowed her breathing to shorten as her muscles threatened to give up. There, she'd done it. A new personal record on that particular machine, although she'd noticed recently, that all the personal bests on the gym equipment now belonged to the Valhallan men, which had caused some discontent among the male bodyguards.

The last two guys using the equipment headed for the locker room, leaving her alone. She turned toward the stationary bike, eager to give her aching arms a short respite before she challenged herself again.

"My lady."

She turned to find Sven watching her, his appreciative gaze fixed on her ass.

"I thought you weren't coming."

Damn, she'd said coming again. Would that word ever stop conjuring up the image of Sven masturbating in the garden?

Sven frowned and checked his wristband. "You said to meet you in the gym at five and here I am. Did I miss something?"

"It's ten past five and you were supposed to meet me in my office."

He planted his hands on his hips.

"But you are not in your office and I'm sure you said to meet in the gym."

Had she said that? A vague memory from the previous night niggled at her.

"I am only here, because you didn't turn up at five."

His frown grew deeper and he stepped closer. "You are just making things difficult. I am here, you are here. What is the problem?"

She resisted an urge to poke him in the chest.

"You are the problem."

"What have I done now?"

"You were supposed to be in my office at five. You didn't appear so I decided to go and do something else with my valuable time. If you wish to liaise with me, may I suggest you turn up on time tomorrow?"

"I am here now."

She glared at him. "I am busy."

A low sound rather like a growl emerged from his mouth.

"Are all the females on the planet as contrary as you and the queen?"

"Probably."

"Then perhaps it is better than Valhalla has less of you rather than more. Between you and the queen, I am struck dumb."

Thea stared at his luscious mouth. "I hadn't noticed."

He ran a hand through his short fox-red hair and sighed. "The king has returned. I had to take care of the baby."

Thea fought a smile. "You did?" She tried to imagine Sven singing lullabies and found it an intriguing image. Could a man as big as he was be that gentle?

"For some reason, I am the only one who can persuade the young prince to go to sleep. I was busy with him when I realized I was late for our meeting."

"And where were the kid's parents during all this?"

"The king and queen were in bed together. The king had much seed to share with his queen."

Thea grimaced. "TMI, Sven."

"What?"

"Too much information."

He reached out and hooked a finger under her chin.

"You do not wish to know that the king and queen mate?"

"Surely that's their business?"

"But if offends you that the king couldn't wait to mate with the queen? He is a lusty man, well suited to the queen's demanding nature. Sometimes they disappear for days until the king is so sated that his seed runs dry."

Thea stared into his brown eyes. How would that feel to make love so many times that you exhausted a man's supply of sperm? She studied Sven speculatively.

"Has that ever happened to you?"

"What?"

Thea licked her lips. "Has your seed ever run dry?"

A flicker of pain darkened his eyes before he dropped his gaze. "Nay, I have not been so honored."

She touched his cheek, felt the soft bristles stirring against her skin, wanted to lick his face and feel them against her tongue. *Damn, stop that.* She wasn't talking to him, was she?

He bent his head, fitted his mouth over hers and kissed her. Her knees started to wobble. He slid his arm around her waist and held her close. His huge erection prodded her stomach.

"I enjoyed your taste, my lady."

"My…taste."

"The taste of your woman's desire. The rich cream between your thighs when you opened them for me."

She pushed at his chest. "Mr. Magnusson, may I remind you that we are at work? I told you, I don't mix business with pleasure."

He tapped his wristband. "It is after five, yes? You are officially off duty."

"No, I'm still on government property and your comments are inappropriate."

He frowned down at her, his arm still firmly around her waist.

"I did not please you?"

"Magnusson…"

His hand slid down over her hip and cupped her sex. "I am distraught. This time I will try harder to make sure you find my attentions enjoyable."

She pulled out of his grasp, her breathing uneven, certain that her cheeks were scarlet.

"Why do men turn everything into a contest?" She glared at Sven. "I'm here to use the gym equipment and then I'm going home—alone."

"I will help you."

"I do not need any help."

He held her gaze, his brown eyes full of sexual challenge.

"But I have been told that it is dangerous to work out alone. Everyone needs a spotter, isn't that so?"

"Only if they use certain machines and I'm going to make certain that I don't use them."

He bowed. "Then I will simply work out alongside you."

Thea let out an aggravated breath as he strolled back toward the changing rooms. Why wouldn't he take no for an answer? Why wouldn't he let her alone? She gazed at the nearest machine. Because she'd dared to question his manliness, of course. What male wouldn't feel the need to prove himself if he felt inadequate?

She sighed and sat down on the bench. She slid her hands into the grips and brought them together in front of her chest. Sweat slid down her face as she worked. The two guys she'd seen earlier appeared from the locker room and went past her with a cheery goodbye.

"Let me help you."

She opened her eyes to find Sven in front of her. His muscular chest was bare as were his legs. He wore the shortest, tightest pair of black workout pants she had ever seen. They looked liked they'd been painted on him and emphasized every curve and bulge of his thighs and groin.

"I'm fine, thank you."

Her rhythm deserted her and she could no longer bring the paddles into her chest. Sven placed his hands over the outside of the paddles, his fingers brushing hers.

Try it now."

With his help, it was almost too easy. Instead of concentrating on her muscles, she watched the concentration on his face as he worked with her. God, he was beautiful, his long eyelashes sweeping down over his eyes as he studied her movements. His unique scent surrounded her, reminding her of the high desert and the exotic perfumes of the night blooming cactus.

She slammed the paddles back and fought to catch her breath.

"I'm done."

He moved closer, trapping her hands in the grips. His mouth descended on hers and he licked the beads of sweat from her lips.

"You are stronger than you look, my lady." He licked her lower lip, worried it with his teeth. "Why do you train like a warrior when you should have a man to defend you?"

She bit his lip and he jerked away.

"Every woman should know how to defend herself. She can't always rely on a man."

He cupped her cheek, his mouth grim. "Why do you say this? Has someone hurt you?"

She tried to smile. "My Mom had a lot of boyfriends. Some of them tried to come onto me. I learned how to defend myself pretty quickly."

"Come onto you?"

"You know, steal a kiss or a grope or worse."

Anger flashed in his eyes and he hissed a curse. "Where was your father? Why didn't he protect you?"

"He was long gone. I don't even know his name. My mom can't remember it either."

His fingers tightened on her jaw.

"How can you smile when you say such terrible things?"

"What do you want me to do? Cry and give up? I'm not that kind of woman."

He stepped back, the emotion in his eyes almost too intense for her to deal with. She shrugged.

"Sven? It's okay. None of them raped me or anything."

He bowed his head, his hands clenched into fists at his sides. Thea stood up.

"I need to get on."

He moved to one side and she immediately missed the heat from his body. As she brushed past him he caught her hand and kissed it.

"Perhaps you are right to train your body. On this world, most men seem incapable of protecting their womenfolk."

She pushed him gently away. "And they don't have to be. We're all equal. We can all take care of ourselves."

"Like your mother and father took care of you?" He abruptly turned his back on her as if he couldn't bear to see her face. "I'm sorry my lady, but the thought of you being preyed upon by those who should have taken care of you is…distasteful to me."

Eager to give him some space, Thea walked across to another machine and lay back on the bench. It made her uncomfortable to hear Sven's concern for her, especially as she'd managed to convince herself that she was way beyond her crappy upbringing and a different person now.

After a vocal command, the machine lowered a bar loaded with the weight she specified and she grasped it with both hands. She took several long slow breaths before even daring to try to press the bar upward. Sweat trickled down between her shoulder blades making her back stick to the plastic-covered bench. A shadow over her head made her pause.

"It's all right, my lady. I'll just watch."

She gripped the bar more firmly and straightened her arms until her elbows locked and the bar remained stationary above her. After three seconds she lowered it and then repeated the motion five more times. When the bar lifted at her request to add more weight, Sven moved to stand at the bottom of the bench.

"It would help if I stabilized your hips and back."

She studied him carefully. "Why?"

He shrugged. "Because then you could lift more weight and beat your personal record."

The bar returned and she grasped it. She'd seen some of the other guys use that trick. "Okay then, but don't distract me."

"Why would I do that? I only wish to be of service."

She shivered as his big hands curved around her hips holding her pinned firmly to the bench. To her surprise it did seem easier to lift. After three more weight increases, she ordered the bar away and looked down at him. He sat on the end of the bench, his gaze fixed on her pussy, his fingers massaging the flesh at her hips.

"Sven, I'm done. You can let go now."

He shook his head. "Did you know that the skimpy garment you are wearing has exposed almost all of your pussy to me?"

Thea tried to slow her breathing as one of his hands left her hip, trailed over her stomach and between her legs.

"It's for exercise. No one cares."

His thumb settled over her clit. "I bet the other men working out here enjoy seeing you half-exposed, warm and sweating. I bet they would like to touch you like this."

She shivered as he stroked the damp cloth over her clit and it swelled to his touch.

"All I need to do is hook one finger under this tiny piece of cloth and I'd be inside you." He shifted back on the bench until she felt his hot breath on her parted thighs, the slight scratch of his unshaven cheek against her skin. "Would you like that, my lady? Would you like to feel the length of my cock thrusting inside you?"

He started to lick the now-sodden fabric, his tongue gradually working over her clit until his teeth closed around it. She couldn't stop her hips coming up off the bench in a desperate bid to keep him touching her. One long finger slid inside her and she bit her lip. What was it about him that made her so desperate for his touch? She'd been ready for him all day, her whole body poised to explode.

"You are very wet, my lady. I think you would take my cock easily."

She closed her eyes as he began to work his finger in and out of her in a slow, slick rhythm that edged her closer and closer toward a climax. His tongue continued to suck strongly at her clit, driving her wild. He was more direct than any lover she'd ever had before, his focus entirely on her sexual pleasure. Perhaps that was why she responded to him so quickly. She no longer cared if anyone walked in on them. She no longer cared that she was at work, only that he finish what he had started the night before and fill her with his cock.

"Thea…"

His hand crept up to her breast, squeezed her already taut nipple and then pinched it hard.

"Thea, we cannot do this here. Let me take you home."

She grabbed hold of his arm and dug her nails into his skin. He gave a muffled grunt, his face now buried in her pussy.

"Don't you dare stop! If you don't make me come right this minute, I'll castrate you, Sven Magnusson, and you won't have to worry about getting between my legs ever again."

She gasped as he settled his teeth on her clit and shoved all four fingers inside her. She climaxed with a scream, her thighs gripped his head, determined to stop him from moving anywhere until she finished enjoying the best orgasm of her life.

Sven tried to gulp in some air but all that did was make him suck in more of Thea's cream. He swallowed it gladly, murmured his approval against her most intimate flesh until she relaxed her death grip on his head. He straightened his arms and pushed away from her. His cock ached so ferociously that he wanted to rip off his shorts and bury himself deep inside her until she came again and allowed him his release.

She lay back on the bench, her eyes closed, her breathing so rapid he could see the rise and fall of her breasts. He groaned as her erect nipples beckoned his mouth and his fingers. He prayed for the resolution to resist and muttered.

"I am going to shower."

Her eyes flicked open and she blushed a deep fiery red.

"Tell me, no one saw us."

"My lady, my head was between your thighs, what do you think I could see apart from your swollen wet pussy?"

He climbed off the bench and frowned down at her. Was she embarrassed by his attentions? He'd been the one trying to stop, not her. Her gaze fell to his shorts and she licked her lips. He stepped back. If she touched him now he'd explode like an inexperienced boy. He took a deep breath.

"I am going to shower."

He walked off toward the changing rooms, one hand cupped carefully around his engorged cock. He let out his breath as the door swung shut behind him and headed to the shower. While the water heated, he returned to the locker room for a towel and the dubious pleasure of trying to remove his skin-tight shorts without making himself come.

He started to pull them down, wincing as the dripping crown of his cock was revealed in all its swollen purple glory. The door opened and he froze, hand over his partially uncovered cock.

"I can help you with that."

He found himself unable to move as Thea came in and went down on her knees in front of him. She touched his thigh and he shuddered.

"You keep walking away from me, Sven. Why do you do that?"

Her fingers trailed up his thigh and feathered over the bulging fabric of his groin. He caught her hand and bit back a groan as she deliberately squeezed his shaft. She had no idea how much her touch affected him. The continual war within him that yearned for her mouth, for her fingers and the delicate lick of her tongue, yet feared them at the same time. He cleared his throat.

"We are at work?"

"That's my line. Try again."

She pushed his hands away and tugged at the waistband of his shorts. His breath hissed out as she caressed the very tip of his cock.

"You are like the queen," he said hoarsely. "You keep changing your mind about what you want."

She looked up at him, her fingers trapped between his shorts and thick shaft. "A woman is entitled to change her mind if she wants to." She touched the slit of his cock, probed it with her fingernail. "And, quite frankly, having seen this, I believe I *have* to change my mind, take you into my mouth and suck you hard." She pulled roughly at his shorts until they slid off his ass. "Do you have a problem with that?"

Sven shook his head. Speech required intelligence and all the blood in his brain had deserted to his cock. He stifled a groan as her lips closed around his crown. He couldn't stop himself burying one of his hands in her hair, just in case she had any thought of escaping him again. She hummed an approving sound through her nose as her mouth slid lower and lower.

With one desperate tug of his hand, his shorts slid down to his knees. She cupped his balls drawing them tight and high against the base of his shaft. His hand fisted as she began to suck him, the lush sounds and her small noises of enjoyment made him even bigger. He cradled the back of her head in his outstretched fingers, amazed that she was willing to take him so deep and not gag. His hips moved to the rhythm set by her mouth and he gave himself up to the ecstasy of her touch.

"Hard, my lady, I like it hard."

He couldn't stop the plea rising from his lips. He couldn't deny the desire to tell her what he craved, what he needed, what she seemed to understand already. She stopped sucking and he held his breath. Had he destroyed the moment? Did she think he was a deviant? He tensed as she looked up at him.

"It's okay, Sven, I like it hard too."

His breath hissed out as she demonstrated what she meant with her teeth, rougher than the queen had ever been, more demanding than any woman he could remember.

"Thea, I need to come." He tugged on her hair when she didn't answer him. "If you don't want my seed, tell me now."

In response, she sucked harder, her teeth grazing his shaft with every long stroke. He forgot the need for caution and pushed into her willing mouth, his cock hitting the back of her throat with every other thrust. He only just remembered not to shout his excitement out to the world as he climaxed and felt his hot seed spurt down her throat.

When he regained enough breath, Sven looked down. He was trembling like a girl. Thea held his cock in one hand as she licked him clean. Her small tongue darted into every crevice. He cursed as he felt himself twitch and grow again. The queen was the last woman who had touched him like this, made something he'd began to avoid into something pleasurable again. But not like Thea, not this overwhelming sense of rough, sensual satisfaction. His wife hadn't liked to take him in her mouth at all. She'd complained he was too big, but then, she'd been a small woman…

Sven released his grip on Thea's hair and carefully stepped back, letting his cock slide between her fingers. He went down on one knee.

"Thank you, my lady. You do me great honor by accepting my seed."

Thea stood up. Sven had gone all formal on her again. She had the strangest feeling that he was dying to get away from her. Had she committed some unspeakable crime against a Valhallan male by touching him?

"You make everything sound so official."

He looked up at her, his naked body gleaming with sweat. God he was beautiful. Muscles in all the right places and the biggest cock she had ever had the pleasure of taking into her mouth. He frowned.

"I am serious. You gave me great honor."

She shrugged, uncomfortable with the intent look in his eyes. "I gave you a blowjob. Okay, it was a great blowjob but that's all it was."

He got slowly to his feet, his large frame towering over her and folded his arms over his massive chest. She wanted to lick the beads of sweat from his perfect abs.

"So you would do that for any man?"

"Of course not!"

He stepped closer until his toes touched hers. "Then accept my thanks."

"I haven't thanked you for making me come, why should you thank me?"

"I do not need your thanks. It is my responsibility, as a male, to bring you to your pleasure. I do not expect anything in return."

"Yeah, right."

He scowled. "I do not understand that expression. It sounds as if you are agreeing with me, yet I sense it means the opposite."

"Don't they have sarcasm on Valhalla?"

She glared right back at him, deliberately pushing her breasts against his lightly haired chest. Her nipples hardened instantly and she bit back a moan. He breathed out, making the situation worse.

"Thea, I am trying to behave like an honorable man."

"What exactly is that supposed to mean?"

"On my planet, a male only mates fully with his wife."

Thea smiled. "You're kidding, right? Are you trying to tell me that you go into marriage as a virgin? Because I have to say, Sven, that you didn't seem very virginal when you used your mouth on me."

He ran a hand through his thick auburn hair. "No, you misunderstand me. There are very few women on Valhalla. All males are expected to learn how to please a woman in all ways."

"Are you serious?" Hastily, Thea blinked away a whole series of salacious images that flashed through her mind. "But what happens if you don't find a mate? Don't you ever get to have sex?"

He dropped his gaze to her breasts and sighed.

"Thea...I have to shower."

He turned away to remove his shorts, displaying his tight muscled ass. As she watched him struggle to kick off the tight fabric, a pulse throbbed incessantly between her legs.

"Sven, tell me the truth. You have had sex, haven't you?"

"Only with one woman."

"You're kidding me, right?"

He threw his shorts to the ground, grabbed a towel and walked out on her.

Again.

Chapter Five

ഌ

"Sven, is something wrong?"

Sven looked over his shoulder to where Douglass the queen lounged on the bed feeding her son. The king sat behind her, his fond gaze on his child and his wife. It was after eleven at night and Harlan and Bron were in the gym working out. In Sven's present state, the intimate picture the king and queen presented was almost too much to bear.

He forced a smile. "There is nothing wrong, My Queen. I am simply thinking about our trip home."

Douglass sighed. "I'm so looking forward to going back. I can't wait to start all my new programs for women."

Sven met Marcus' bland gaze and looked swiftly away. The king cleared his throat.

"I am sure the women of Valhalla will be delighted to see you, my love."

Douglass frowned up at the king. "I know you think most of my ideas are nuts, but at least let me try to convince your women that they don't have to be fought over by idiot males or live like brood mares."

"I'm not stopping you, am I?" The king kissed the top of her head. "And I believe we were trying to talk about what ailed Sven rather than start yet another spirited discussion about the wrongs done to Valhalla's females."

"Yes, Sven. What is it? You don't seem to be at all happy. Are you homesick?"

Sven sighed. The queen was tenacious when roused. "I miss Valhalla and aye, I'm looking forward to going home."

"But that's not the problem, right?" Douglass handed the baby to the king who winked at Sven, draped his son over his shoulder and started rubbing his back.

Sven stared at them. What could he say? That he lusted after another woman so badly that his cock was permanently hard and his dreams filled with images of her under him being fucked in every position possible? He cleared his throat.

"Sometimes I find it difficult to understand the mating rituals of your planet, My Queen."

Douglass crossed her legs and sat up. "There is a woman you are interested in?" She snapped her fingers in the king's direction. "See? I told you he was in love."

"No, I'm in lust." Sven shot to his feet and bowed. "I wish to bed this female and yet, in my heart I know it would be wrong."

Marcus swung around to stare at Sven.

"My wife tells me that it's not considered wrong to make love to a woman you are not married to on Earth."

Sven glowered at the king. "And you think that makes it right?"

"That is not what I said. I merely suggested that women here don't expect a marriage ring before they take a lover. Remember there are more women on Earth than men. Most people prefer to try out several lovers before choosing the one they wish to mate with."

"And because we happen to be stuck here, you are suggesting I ignore the values I was brought up with and fuck as many women as I like?"

Douglass slid off the bed and came to stand in front of Sven, her eyes blazing. She poked him hard in the chest.

"Don't talk to your king like that. Of course Marcus is not suggesting you go out and fuck anything female. He's merely trying to tell you that if there is a woman here who you think you might come to care for, take the opportunity to get to know her and, if she offers to take you to bed, do it!"

Sven took a step back and bowed his head. "But what about you? I meant no offence. I am one of your pleasure servers. How can I serve you and yet desire another?"

The queen's gaze softened and she touched his cheek. "If you can find a meaningful sexual relationship with a woman you love, go for it. How could I deny you something I have myself?"

Marcus came up and put his hand on the queen's shoulder. "Douglass is right. Neither of us would wish to deprive you of the joy of a true mate."

Sven looked helplessly into the king's eyes. "But what if I want her to be my true mate and she refuses me?"

Marcus laughed. "Worry about that when you get there."

Sven wristband beeped and he checked the message. "I have to go. There is a security alert on the perimeter wall. I will consider everything you have told me."

Marcus handed Sven the baby. "Give my son to his nurse for a nap. All this talk about mating has made me eager for the queen." He winked at his wife. "I did tell you that I wanted at least ten children, didn't I?"

Sven exited as swiftly as he could before he heard the queen's indignant reply. He handed the prince over to his nurse and made his way swiftly into the palace gardens. His security system showed a lone figure moving steadily toward the house from the direction of the apple orchards.

He paused to listen by the high orchard wall, aware that if he kept going he was on a collision course with the intruder. This was one of the weak spots in the security system he had been discussing with Matt on the previous day. He tensed as a figure appeared at the exit to the orchard. In the moonlight he could only see the shadow of the man's face and the glint of the high powered camera attached to his right hand.

Sven stepped behind the guy and brought his arm around his neck.

"Do not resist and you will be fine." He grunted as the man tried to kick him and simply tightened his grip. "You are trespassing on Valhallan property."

"Get your filthy hands off me!"

Sven chuckled as he turned the man around to face him.

"My hands are clean but I am quite happy to stain them with your blood."

"Christ, you're huge."

The guy's mouth opened as his gaze traveled up the length of Sven's body to his face.

"I am also angry. I do not like my king and queen's peace to be disturbed."

He pushed the reporter back against the wall and searched him for weapons.

"I'm Mick Jarvis, reporter with the *Daily Scream*, the best entertainment show on the holo-tube."

Sven extracted an expensive communication device from Jarvis' pocket.

"I do not watch entertainment. I prefer to make my own."

"But you're from Valhalla, right? You're one of the hunky bodyguards. Can't you just give me five minutes of your time to tell our watchers what it's really like inside that sex-mad kingdom? I hear your queen likes a bit of variety in her sex life."

Sven stopped his search to gaze down at Mick Jarvis' animated face.

"I do not understand what you are talking about. All I intend to do is walk you back to the security gate, and allow your Earth police to take care of you. Unfortunately I am not allowed to kill or dismember you as is traditional for trespassers on Valhalla."

Mick gave a nervous laugh. "That's a joke, right?"

"I never joke, especially about the reputation of my queen." Sven shoved him toward the main gate, careful to keep an eye on the man's camera. Mick Jarvis kept talking.

"If you can just answer a few questions for me."

"No, I cannot."

Sven spoke into his wristband, saw the guards fanning out to meet him in the pool of light around the security center. All the good humor fled from Mick's face as he grabbed Sven's arm.

"I know what's going on. Whether you cooperate or not, I'll make sure you look real bad."

Sven handed the man back his communication device and straightened his sleeve.

"Do what you must, but be very sure you are willing to face the consequences."

Mick laughed. "Oh don't worry about that. I'm a lot tougher than you think."

Sven watched as the Earth security team surrounded the reporter and took him back to the gate. What was Mick hinting at? They had been very careful to appear as simply the queen's bodyguards and not her pleasure servers. Had someone seen something they shouldn't?

"Mr. Magnusson?"

He looked down to find Adams, the security team leader beside him.

"Do you want me to notify Ms. Cooper of the security infringement? She does like to be kept informed."

Sven smiled into the darkness. "It's all right. I'll tell her myself."

It seemed the compulsion to go to her was strong enough to overcome his scruples. Before he could change his mind, he grabbed his leather coat and arranged for transport. Bron and Harlan were on duty tonight. As long as he returned by dawn he wouldn't be missed.

Thea yawned at the salacious images on the holo-screen. Why did her favorite erotic movie suddenly seem so boring? The two men looked too thin and scrawny to service the woman who was designed to look like her. What the heroine needed was a big, strong virile, intergalactic Viking or two inside her.

Her wrist unit buzzed making her jump. Sven's unsmiling face appeared in the view screen.

"My lady, there has been another security breech. I am bringing you my report."

"In person?"

Thea squeaked and leapt off the bed. Her bedroom carpet was littered with candy wrappers and an abandoned tub of ice cream. After her frustrating sexual interlude with Sven, she'd come home to try all the old standard remedies to make herself feel better. Erotic movies, ice cream, her pleasure device; nothing had relieved the ache between her thighs and the almost physical longing to be fucked hard by a real live man.

And now that man was here, outside her door, waiting to be let in. She smoothed her hair down with trembling fingers. If she let him in her apartment they would have sex. Did she really want that? *Oh god, yes please.*

She opened the door. He filled the frame, his black leather coat unbuttoned to display his white open-necked shirt and tight leather pants. She continued to stare up at him as he slowly took off his sunglasses. His gaze flicked down her body.

"May I enter?"

"Of course, come on in."

She stepped back and crossed her arms over her chest, suddenly aware that she wore only a thin silk nightshirt. Her nipples were already hard just from looking at him fully clothed. He stepped into her apartment which seemed to shrink around her until there was barely enough air to breathe. She gestured at his coat.

"Do you want to take that off?"

He smiled down at her as he removed his coat and laid it over the back of the couch. She reached out a hand to smooth the soft warm leather.

"So what happened at the compound that made it necessary for you to come all this way to see me?"

His eyebrow rose. "Yesterday you told me that I was to keep you informed of every security breach, however minor. I am simply obeying your orders."

"Was anyone hurt?"

"No. I managed to restrain myself this time."

Thea stared at him. "You could have told me about this over the com-link."

He stepped closer until she had to raise her chin to look into his eyes.

"Com-links can be tampered with. I wanted to make sure you got the message. The man I apprehended gave me his name and the gossip rag he works for. I wanted to know if he was familiar to you."

"Who was it?" Damn, it was hard to think when Sven was so close.

"A man named Mick Jarvis from the *Daily Scream*."

"That guy is a pain in the ass. He's known for breaking every civilized rule of privacy. You didn't hurt him did you?"

"As I said, I restrained myself, although his insinuations were enough to make my blood boil."

Thea held Sven's gaze. "Mick Jarvis is a dangerous guy. Keep away from him."

The corner of Sven's mouth kicked up.

"Are you worried about my safety, my lady? He would not best me in a fight."

"He wouldn't fight fair. He'd use anything he could get against you."

Sven frowned. "Then what can we do?"

Thea pushed a hand through her hair. "Nothing at the moment. Unless he turns up again or prints something outrageous."

"Your planet lacks a good judicial system."

"Innocent until proven guilty doesn't work for you?"

Sven turned away to pace the room and was brought up short by the couch. "On Valhalla, the man would be incarcerated and sent before the king who would dispense justice."

"And one man is more able to judge correctly than a jury of his peers?"

Sven swung around to glower at her. "If the man is worthy of his kingship, then yes."

"Well, whatever you think, we're on Earth and the home team rules apply."

"The home team?"

"Let's just say, Earth has the advantage on this one."

Sven sighed. "It is difficult to protect my king and queen when I do not fully understand your culture. I will be glad when we are back on Valhalla."

"Really." Thea walked toward the front door and grabbed the handle. "Well off you go, then. If everything is so much better on Valhalla, you'd better scurry off back to the palace where you can feel comfortable."

"I do not scurry."

Sven followed her, reached over her head and held the door shut.

"There are some things I would miss."

"Like what?"

He leaned closer until his lips brushed her hair.

"The game of football, the taste of pizza...you."

She tried to shrug. "I come in third behind pizza? Wow thanks."

He kissed her forehead, then nuzzled her nose. "The scent of your woman's pleasure, the feel of your mouth around my cock." He kissed her cheek, nipped at her lower lip. "My cock filling you."

Thea found herself leaning into him, her hand curving around his neck.

"You haven't filled me with your cock."

His tongue slid into her mouth and she forgot to breathe as he explored her with a sensitivity she would never have imagined he possessed. When she opened her eyes, she was in his arms, one of her hands wrapped in his thick red hair, the other on his shoulder.

She whimpered as his big hands roamed over her body, slipping under her nightshirt, pressing her against him, making her aware of every inch of his big hard cock. She pulled at his shirt, desperate to touch his skin. His fingers connected with her naked ass and cupped her cheeks.

Thea pulled hard on Sven's hair until he was forced to look up at her.

"If you stay, you have to finish this time." She said fiercely. "No walking away from me, do you understand?"

"I understand my lady. I would be honored to share your bed."

He dropped to his knees, kissed the swell of her mound through the already damp satin. His tongue coaxed her clit into swelling and showing through the fabric. Thea gasped and shook his shoulder.

"Come to bed with me, now."

Sven stumbled to his feet and followed her through to her bedroom. Thea groaned silently when she realized she'd left the holo-movie on. Sven strode up to the screen, crushing the wrappers and the ice cream tub underfoot as he passed.

"This woman looks like you."

"Well that's because she's supposed to be me."

Sven swung around and glowered at her. "You share your lovemaking with everyone?"

"Of course I don't!"

He jabbed one finger at the screen. "This is an entertainment system. According to the queen, everyone on Earth has one; therefore everyone can see you having sex."

Thea bit her lip. "Sven, I'm not appearing in a porno movie or anything."

He folded his arms across his massive chest. "I do not understand."

"Don't you have porn on Valhalla?"

"If you mean, do we film ourselves making love and share it with the whole planet, then, no."

"Then how do men and women get off?"

His frown darkened. "Get off what?"

She gestured at his groin. "You know, when they masturbate, how do they stimulate themselves?"

"Women always have a man available to them. They never need to use other stimulants."

"And how about the men?"

"They might be invited to watch a mating or they are usually expected to help stimulate a woman."

A slow pulse throbbed between Thea's thighs. "You mean everyone learns through personal experience rather than from watching a movie or a holo-show?"

He nodded, his expression still watchful. Thea walked across to touch his arm.

"On this planet, lovemaking is usually a very private thing between two consenting adults. What you see on the screen is my attempt to make up for the fact that I am alone and I still want sex."

He shrugged her hand off. "So you allow your body to be used like this?"

"No, I made this up, purely for myself. It's my own personal fantasy program. I can input any images or scenarios I want and replay them for myself when I'm feeling particularly…horny."

Sven stepped back and stared at the two guys pictured with her image on the screen. "These men do not look worthy of you. This one is too slender and would not be able to wield a broadsword in your defense." He pointed at the younger man. "His cock is small as well. He would hardly give you much pleasure."

Thea fought a smile. "I was thinking about changing the program. How about a nice tall red-haired intergalactic Viking?"

Sven stepped closer and hooked a finger under her chin.

"Surely you would rather follow my planet's example and experience such a man in the flesh?"

Thea inhaled the scent of aroused male and warm leather. She placed her hand over his chest, felt the beat of his heart kick up.

"I'm still not sure if I'm doing the right thing…"

His mouth covered hers, cutting off her doubts and she responded to his kiss, standing on tip toe and wrapping her arms around his neck. He picked her up as if she weighed nothing and held her against him, her sex lined up against the hard ridge of his erection. His hand slid under her nightshirt and stroked her buttocks.

"I want this, Thea. I want to bring you pleasure."

His hoarse words made her writhe against him, plucking at his shirt until he put her down and worked at his belt buckle. He groaned as she tugged on his shirt and drew it over his head. She stopped to admire his muscled chest and tight abs. A slight sheen of sweat covered his golden skin and she leaned in to taste him.

He caught her hands and drew them behind her back.

"There is no need to rush, my lady. I promise I will service you all night."

She held his gaze. "Until you run out of come?"

His pupils dilated until they were almost all black. "If that is your wish." He worked the buttons on her nightshirt free and pushed the silky garment to the floor. With a guttural sigh, he fell to his knees.

"You are beautiful, my lady."

Thea stared down at him, aware of the breadth of his shoulders and the strength of his muscled arms. All at her disposal for one night. Her sex flooded with cream at the thought of him pounding into her.

He leaned forward, licked her mound, sliding his tongue deep into the slit to find her clit. He spread her legs with his hands and delved deeper. She moaned as he lapped at her, the scrape of his stubbled chin a torment against the soft flesh of her inner thighs. His tongue slid further in to caress her sex, rim her opening and stab inside her.

She clutched one hand in his thick red hair, one on his shoulder to steady her body against his sensual onslaught. He murmured his approval against her pussy making her quiver.

"Your body welcomes me. Your sex overflows with cream to ease my way." He slid one thick finger inside her and her muscles tried to clench around it. He laughed softly. "You need more than one finger to satisfy this ache, my lady." He sucked on her clit and pushed two more fingers deep inside.

She gasped and dug her fingernails into his flesh as he started to move his fingers in and out. Each thrust, pushing her up onto her toes, destroying her ability to stand alone, making her clutch onto his broad frame. A climax tore through her and she whimpered, her knees suddenly weak as she leaned into him.

"That was very nice, my lady. But I'm sure you can give me more."

He continued to hold her steady as he got to his feet, his lips shining with her cream. She let him back her up toward the bed and fall down on it with her. He frowned as he rolled to one side.

"What is this?"

He showed her the pink column of her pleasure-stick which she'd left in the bed to help her enjoy the holo-movie. She felt her skin heat with embarrassment.

"Um, it's a pleasure device."

He sat up, his visible erection straining against the front of his leather pants. He examined the pink synthetic tube, turned it on, stroked the pulsating rubbery surface with his fingers. He also opened the bottle of rose-scented lube and squeezed some onto his finger.

Thea leaned toward him. "Don't tell me. You don't have these on Valhalla because every female has plenty of real cocks to choose from."

He smiled at her. "Actually, the king told me about these. He has something similar which he uses with the queen."

She stared down at the throbbing pink shaft. "I don't think we'll need it tonight, will we?"

"If you wish to recreate your fantasy of being penetrated by two cocks at the same time, then it will be very useful."

As he continued to play with the toy, Thea's nipples hardened in a sudden aching rush. He raised one eyebrow.

"That is your wish, is it not? Two men pounding away in you, pouring their cum deep and hot inside you."

She could only nod as he bent to lick her taut nipple. She'd never told anyone about that particular fantasy, the thought of being taken by two men, of being shared between them, of having no choice but to take whatever they gave her. His hand slid over her hip and down to her ass. She shivered as he spread his long fingers over her butt cheeks. The tip of his lubed finger slid inside her ass.

"Have you ever had two men fuck you?"

"Only in my imagination."

He slid his finger in further. "Have you ever taken a man's cock here?"

"Yes." She found herself arching her back, offering herself to him.

"Did you like it?" His finger was in deep now and she made herself relax.

"Yes."

His low growl of approval made her sex clench with anticipation. "Then perhaps we should start here."

While Thea watched him, Sven arranged a stack of pillows in the center of the bed and gently maneuvered her over them, her ass raised by the pillows, her face buried in the sheets. He ran a hand over the soft skin of her buttocks. His cock felt as if it would burst out of his pants at any moment, but he wanted to wait, to make it perfect for her, to give her everything she had ever desired.

Her fantasies about being fucked by more than one man had aroused him even further. She was better suited to a life on Valhalla than she realized. He couldn't help wondering how she would react to him bringing Harlan and Bron to her bed. Would she enjoy the experience of being pleasured by three men or find it too overwhelming?

He bent to lick her pussy, circling his tongue over the tight bud of her ass until it yielded to his touch . He coated two of his fingers with more lube and slid them inside her. She arched up against his touch pushing him deeper making him groan. He scissored his fingers, widening her passage for the impending thickness of his cock.

"Do you like that, my lady?"

She moaned, her hips rolling as he pleasured her. He added two more oil-soaked fingers, felt her relax and accept him. With his free hand he scooped up her pleasure device and set it on a low pulse.

"Although I do not have two cocks to pleasure you with, I can fill you with this while I fuck your ass."

He leaned forward and bit Thea's shoulder, felt her quiver, licked and soothed the small mark he'd made. Lust shivered through him as he removed his fingers from her ass and slowly undid his leather pants, letting them drop to the floor. His breath hissed out as his weeping throbbing shaft jutted straight out from his groin. He ran a hand over his heated flesh, coating himself in oil and pre-cum.

As he aligned the head of his cock with her ass and began to penetrate her, he used his other hand to slide the pleasure-device into her pussy. Holding his breath, he slid home, keeping the same slow pace for both his cock and the sex toy. His balls lodged against her and he sighed. She was so tight, his cock was being squeezed almost to the point of pain.

He crouched over her, one hand cupping the pleasure-device, his fingers dancing over her clit, the other planted on the bed beside them as leverage.

The last person he'd touched like this had been the queen when she'd honored him by accepting his cock in her time of separation from the king. It had only happened once but Sven thought it had been his finest moment—until now. Thea felt amazing. Every thick inch of his cock was jammed inside her. She was so tight, he could feel the steady pulse of the pleasure device in her channel reverberating through his shaft.

He started to rock his hips, the oil and his extreme excitement easing his way. Thea moaned with each solid thrust, her body moving with him, urging him on. He gritted his teeth, determined to make her come before he did, although his years without penetrative sex made it difficult. His heart thudded in his chest as she spasmed and screamed beneath him. He increased his pace, losing his rhythm as he thrust into her, barely remembering to keep his weight off her slim form as she climaxed again.

Sensation knotted at the base of his spine and he started to come. Long hot urgent spasms of his seed, deep within her ass. He kept thrusting, shoving himself as deep as he could, desperate to fill her, make her his woman until the only thing she craved was his scent and his cum. It took all his energy to remember to remove the vibrator before he collapsed over her, covering her completely with his body.

After a long while, he managed to roll off her and lay on his back, staring up at the ceiling. He couldn't think about what he'd done yet, he could barely manage to breathe. Thea slid off the pillows and arranged herself on his chest. He brought his arm around her and held her close.

"Thank you, my lady. That was excellent."

Her answering chuckle was muffled by his chest. "Thank you. That was awesome."

He found himself smiling. "Better than your previous lovers?"

She sat up and punched his chest. "You are so conceited."

He narrowed his eyes. "But I was better, yes?"

"You were…adequate."

With a roar he sat up and dragged her beneath him. "I fear adequate will not suffice for me tonight. I will strive to be better."

Thea gazed up into his stern face, willing herself not to laugh at his offended expression. He was covered in a fine sheen of sweat which made his muscled physique even more obvious. His cock was already filling out again. What did he expect her to say? That he'd rocked her world? That she'd seen stars, rainbows and untold universal wonders? Well, she had, but he didn't need to know that—yet. She wasn't going to think about any of the emotional girly stuff now, she was going to simply enjoy. Tomorrow was soon enough for the angst. But, he was so perfect…

She touched his flat stomach, felt his abs clench beneath the surface of his skin. God he was beautiful naked. There should be a law that men like him were not allowed to wear clothes — ever.

"If you intend to be better, go and wash up, then come back and try again. I'll wait."

"You will regret toying with me, Thea. I will make you beg for my cock before we are through."

He growled low in his throat and climbed off the bed. While he used the bathroom, she took the opportunity to check in her bedside drawer for a can of *Sperm Be-Gone*. She frowned as she checked the date on the can. How long had it been since she'd used this spray on a man? She hoped it was still in date. Sven's shadow loomed over her.

"What is that? Another toy?"

Thea held out the can. "It's for your cock."

Sven glanced at the gaudy can and then down at his erection. "I do not understand."

Thea shook the can. "This stuff coats your cock and stops you impregnating me."

"Why would you wish me to use that?"

"Because I don't want a baby."

He sat down on the edge of the bed, one hand wrapped around the base of his cock. "Ah, my queen told me about this. It is a form of contraception, yes?"

"That's right. It's much better than the old-fashioned sheaths which basically tried to stop your semen getting inside me, not always successfully." She pointed at the can. "This stuff allows you to ejaculate normally but sterilizes your sperm as they pass through the coating. One spray works all night."

Sven still looked dubious. "It is difficult for me to understand this, my lady. On my planet, every woman is desperate to conceive."

Somehow Thea doubted that. She allowed the can to fall on the rumpled bed. "On this planet it happens to be the direct opposite. If you can't accept that, then we can't make love." She held her breath, aware of a strange feeling of hurt inside her. Was she only desirable if she could become pregnant? He met her gaze, his brown eyes open and direct.

"I would consider myself a lucky man if you allowed me to impregnate you."

She tried to laugh but the sound stuck in her throat as she registered his sincerity. "Thank you, I think, but I'm not changing my mind. No *Sperm Be-Gone*, no sex."

He sighed and reached for the can. "Then I will honor your request my lady."

Sven allowed Thea to direct him as he sprayed the fine mist over his cock and balls. A curious tingling sensation made his shaft jerk and stiffen as the mist settled on his aroused flesh. He sucked in a breath.

"Thor's Bones! This stuff grips my cock like a woman's channel."

Thea knelt beside him, her smile smug. "I told you it would be okay. Apparently it's quite a pleasurable sensation."

Sven watched in fascination as a drop of pre-cum emerged from the crown of his cock. Before it slid down his shaft, he caught it between his finger and thumb. "My seed really can penetrate the barrier."

Thea leaned forward and licked his fingers, her tongue a hard sharp point. "Mmm...I'd say so."

With a growl, Sven pressed her down onto the bed and spread her legs with his knees. "I think you should take more of me than that little drop, my lady. I think you should take all of my cum."

He gripped his cock at the base and guided it toward her pussy. She was already wet and swollen, her clit visible between her puffed up labia. He nudged her clit with the tip of his cock, back and forth, applying a little more pressure every time. Her hands slid up his arms and gripped his biceps. Bending his head, he licked her right nipple in the same slow tempo, continuing the dual torment until she began to writhe and dig her nails into his flesh.

"Please, Sven. Put it inside me, please."

He shifted his hips, allowed the first inch of his thick cock to penetrate her slick wet opening. Despite using the pleasure device, she was still tight. He held still, relishing the slight grip of her sex on his crown. The ache to drive inside her hard and fast was almost unbearable, but it was years since he had been inside a woman's most prized channel and he intended to make every moment last. He placed his hands flat on the bed and straightened his arms.

Thea lay beneath him, legs spread wide, her nipples and mouth reddened from his kisses, her pussy open and wet for him. A strange aching sensation unfurled inside his chest. By Thor, she was the most beautiful female he had ever seen. He looked down to where their bodies were joined, traced the line of his shaft and rimmed the place he filled her.

"More, Sven. Give me more."

He slid in another inch, felt her inner muscles grip his hardened flesh and undulate around him, pulling him deeper and deeper. With a groan, he surged forward until his entire cock was buried to the balls. She took him all, swallowed him up and climaxed immediately.

Sven closed his eyes and gritted his teeth as she came, her soft wild cries ringing in his ears as he fought the desire to pound into her and flood her with his seed. He waited until she stopped pulsing and then drew his cock back until it was barely inside her again. She tried to follow him off the bed but he gripped her hips and held her still.

"If you want me all night, my lady, you need to be patient."

Her eyes narrowed. "Patience is not one of my virtues, Magnusson."

"Then perhaps it is time you learned some."

He rocked his hips, allowing only the first three inches of his cock to penetrate her in a shallow upward motion. She clung onto his forearms and tried to claw her way up but he wouldn't allow that. He held her pinned to the bed. The slick sound of his cock sliding in and out of her and the creak of the bed mirrored her soft panting breaths. Sven gave himself up to the rhythm and angled her hips to find that small nub of flesh inside her that would bring her the greatest pleasure.

He smiled as her breathing became more erratic and her channel tightened and tightened around him as he pressed against her most sensuous flesh.

"See? You are learning already, my lady. After you come for me a few more times I will consider giving you more of my cock."

"I'm not…coming. Oh dammit!"

She climaxed again and he closed his eyes to enjoy the sensation to the fullest. All those years of watching others experience this joy, of wondering if he would ever be worthy to make love again and now he had the chance. Would she always be wet for him like this? Eager for his touch, willing to take him whenever he wanted her? He drew his hips back even further, so only the crown of his cock lay inside her. She was so wet now that he could easily fit inside her if he chose. He kept his strokes shallow and unhurried until she grabbed two handfuls of his hair and pulled hard.

"Give me more, you arrogant, conceited oaf!"

He ripped his head free of her hands and pulled out completely. Her struggles made him harder and more determined to give her everything she desired, even if it left him bloodied and exhausted. Before she could say a word, he got off the bed and went to one of the open drawers in her vanity. He grabbed a couple of silk stockings and returned to straddle her.

"What do you think you are doing?"

"If you still have breath to order me around, I am not doing my job properly."

Excitement flashed in her eyes, reigniting the edgy desire in him. He'd never felt so free with a woman before, so certain that she would respond to his intense sexual demands. With great care, he wrapped the first stocking around her wrists in a loop and tied a knot, trapping her hands together.

"The king tells me that the only way he can get the queen to pay attention to him sometimes is by tying her down on the bed." He attached the other end of the stocking to the headboard, drawing her arms above her head. "Perhaps the same tactics will work for you."

Thea stared up at him, her heart thumping so hard in her chest that she knew he must see her agitation. The raised position of her arms made her breasts jut out, as if begging for his touch. Sven fingered the other stocking, his calm expression belying the urgent thrust of his cock which almost reached his navel. She couldn't move off the bed because of the weight of his muscular body, she could only glare up at him showing him she wasn't scared at all, that she craved everything he was going to do to her.

"I could tie your legs to the corners of the bed, but I think I'll leave them free for the moment."

He plucked at her nipples, pulling at them until they were hard aching points and then licked each one until she was writhing against her bounds. She gasped as he drew one hard point into his mouth and sucked hard. He knelt back, his gaze fixed on her mouth.

"Perhaps I should use the stocking to cover your mouth but I love to hear you scream and beg." He shifted closer until his knees rested on either side of her upper torso. "I also love you sucking my cock." She tensed as he gripped his shaft and brought the crown toward her lips, soaking them in his pre-cum, swallowed hard, enjoying his taste, anticipating his next move.

"I'd like to fuck your mouth now, but I think your pussy needs me more."

In one swift motion, he moved back, grabbed her ankles and brought them over his shoulders. She screamed as he thrust the full length of his thick cock inside her, filling her completely. She couldn't move as his hands steadied on her hips and kept her chained to his pistoning shaft. He kept up a fast deep rhythm that concentrated the weight of his pelvis on her clit and made her come repeatedly. He didn't let up and she almost forgot to breathe as her pleasure reached heights she hadn't believed existed.

He groaned in time to each heavy stroke, slamming into her without restraint and Thea gloried in every rough, erotic moment. This overloading of sensations was just what she needed. Suddenly all her previous lovers seemed inadequate and too sensitive. Sven's movements became shallower and less controlled. He started to tremble.

"By Odin, I'm coming!" He roared as his hot cum flooded her pussy, making her climax again and again.

When Thea came to her senses, Sven lay heavily over her, his breathing as ragged as her own, his face buried in the pillows beside her head. She turned and kissed his ear.

"Untie my hands. I want to touch you."

He pulled out and rolled over to look at her. He kissed the tip of her breast and touched her still swollen clit. She bit her lip as he gently caressed her.

"Thank you, my lady."

She frowned at him. "Set me free and I'll thank you right back."

He shook his head as he made a place for himself between her legs "I haven't finished with you, yet." He bent to kiss her wet sex. "I intend to lick you clean, and ready you for my cock again."

"You aren't going to fall asleep?"

He frowned. "Not until you are completely satisfied, my lady. That would be inexcusable. I will provide you with all the sex you need."

Thea's body immediately heated up again and she relaxed back on the pillows. He was the first man she'd ever been with who had wanted more than a couple of rounds of sex. He made her feel like her sexual needs were totally understandable. With a delicious sigh, she regarded Sven's already half-erect cock. It was definitely going to be a night to remember for both of them…

Chapter Six

෨

Before he closed the bedroom door, Sven took one last look back at Thea. She lay sprawled face down on the bed, her flushed face buried in the pillow, one arm flung out toward where he had slept beside her. She was truly beautiful. He couldn't wait to tell her that he wanted her to be his one true mate. His cock stirred as he thought about waking her with his mouth on her sex.

He reluctantly closed the door, headed back down the stairs and out into the cold unwelcoming fog of a San Francisco summer morning. To his surprise, one of the black embassy vehicles waited in front of the building. The driver got out when he saw Sven.

"Mr. Magnusson? The king and queen require your presence."

Sven's mind ran through a thousand unpleasant scenarios as he hurried to get into the vehicle.

"Is there something wrong with the young prince?"

"Not as far as I know, sir."

Sven stared at the road ahead, willing himself back at the Valhallan residence. He would never forgive himself if something had happened on the only night he wasn't at his post. He barely remembered to thank the driver before he ran up the steps to the royal quarters, forgot the security code and banged on the door instead.

Harlan opened it, his expression grave.

"Sven, I'm glad you're back. The king and queen are in here."

Sven marched toward the royal couple's bedroom.

"What is going on?"

Harlan ran a hand through his long uncombed hair. His eyes were shadowed, his mouth a hard line. "The king will tell you."

"Ah, Sven, come in and shut the door behind you."

Sven halted on the threshold. The king and queen were sitting beside the fire. Bron stood watch over the little prince's cradle. Everyone seemed unharmed; everything was the same although their expressions were grim.

"We have a problem." Douglass stood up and passed a sheaf of papers across to Sven who sat opposite the king. "I was sent these by an anonymous source. Apparently we are going to feature on an exposé story on tonight's *Daily Scream* show."

Sven met her gaze. "I caught a reporter from that show last night. His name was Mick Jarvis. He made some threats about exposing our secrets."

The king's expression was grim. "Well it appears he followed through."

Sven squinted at the blurry images captured on the page in front of him. They'd obviously been shot from long range.

"It is almost impossible to tell exactly what I'm supposed to be looking at."

The queen leaned over his shoulder and jabbed her finger into the center of the page. "Let me help you. This is a picture of you, Harlan, Bron and me, cavorting naked in my bedroom while the king was away last month."

Sven looked at the furious king and chose his words with unusual care. "Sire, you know that we only touch the queen under your express orders?"

Marcus grunted. "I'm not blaming you for pleasuring My Queen. I trust you all implicitly."

Sven felt a twinge of guilt as he remembered the incredible sex he'd just shared with Thea. He gave the papers back to the queen. "I'll find Jarvis, rip out his still beating heart and bring it to you on a platter."

"Thanks for the thought, but I don't think that will help." Douglass perched on the king's broad thigh and he wrapped his arm around her waist. "Marcus, maybe you should keep out of it and let me take the blame. The media here already think the worst of me, a package delivery person, daring to marry a king, so why not let them continue to do so? We'll be back on Valhalla soon."

Sven bowed. "With all due respect, My Queen, I doubt the king would agree to that."

"You are correct."

Douglass sighed and turned to the king. "Marcus…I'm only trying to protect you. This is my planet and my problem. I'm the one who should have made sure our suite was secure before allowing anything of a sexual nature to happen."

He caught her chin in his fingers. "You are my wife and the mother of my child. Do you think I will allow anyone to speak disparagingly of you? Our customs may be different from those of Earth but we are still entitled to our privacy."

"The fault is mine, Sire." Sven stood up. "I am in charge of the queen's security and I failed to protect her. If anyone should take the blame, it is me."

The king held his gaze. "Sit down. There is no blame to be shared. The queen warned me many times that some of the Earth media will stop at nothing to get a good story. She believed it was only a mater of time before our unusual arrangements were discovered."

Harlan shifted in his seat. "I think we should share this information with our Earth security counterparts. They have more experience in dealing with the media here than we do. They might be able to suggest ways to get rid of the problem."

The king nodded. "Sven, set up a meeting in two Earth hours." He mock-scowled at the queen. My wife needs to feed our son and then I need to remind her that I will never let her stand alone."

The queen blushed as the king swept her into his arms. "You don't need to convince me of anything, Marcus. I always believe in you."

"Then show me…"

He kissed her cheek and threw her onto the bed. Sven and the others were already moving toward the door when he climbed on top of her.

Bron shut the door firmly behind them.

"Do you think I should bring the baby?"

Sven glanced back at the royal apartment. "I'm sure they'll hear him if they wake him up."

Bron nodded. "That is true. The queen certainly lets her pleasure be known but the young prince is louder."

Harlan punched Sven's shoulder. "Did you have a pleasant night?"

Sven moved away and crossed to the window. The sun was beginning to appear through the thick drifting mist. "Leave it, Harlan."

"Why? Just because matters have become complicated, doesn't mean we can't celebrate the end of your celibacy. It's scarcely your fault that your night off coincided with a breach of security."

Sven turned around and glared at the two other men.

Harlan raised his eyebrows. "Are you not going to share the details? Bron and I have been celibate too."

"I do not wish to share."

"She was unwilling, then?"

"Nay, she was…" Sven scowled at Harlan's triumphant smile. "She was everything a male could wish for. She honored me."

Harlan opened his mouth but Sven took a threatening step toward him. "That is all I have to say on the matter. Now let us discuss how we are going to explain our 'peculiar' sexual culture to the Earth security team."

Thea glanced at her security monitor and moaned. Apparently the Valhallans had called an emergency meeting in ten minutes and she'd just found out about it. She sipped at the boiling coffee she'd managed to acquire on her frantic journey to work. She'd only just arrived at her desk. Exhausted by Sven's vigorous lovemaking, she'd slept in for the first time in her career. There wasn't even time to call Matt and ask him what the hell was going on.

Her night with Sven had been a revelation. In the past, her boyfriends had complained about her high sexual libido and struggled to keep up with her. With Mark, she'd tried hard to conceal her needs, but at the end, he'd insisted that one of the reasons he'd found someone else was because Thea made him feel inadequate. She'd always imagined that it would take more than one man to satisfy her but Sven had proved otherwise. If all the Valhallan men took their sexual duties so seriously, what would it feel like to have all three of the queen's bodyguards giving you their all?

With a resigned sigh, Thea forced more of the coffee down and got her files in order. She had to stop thinking about sex and Sven. She'd had a fabulous night, she was grateful for it but that was all it was. She was long past the age of spinning childish fairy stories about weddings and husbands and red-haired babies. She stared at the manila covers. This meeting couldn't have anything to do with her and Sven spending the night together could it? Was King Marcus enraged that she'd consorted with one of the queen's bodyguards or was it her own department that was causing a problem?

She opened the door and headed for the large conference room. Whatever happened, she wasn't ashamed of what she'd done. Sven was definitely the best lover she'd ever had. She pictured his face as he'd filled her with his cock, the depth of desire tinged with lust in his brown eyes when she'd come for him. The way he'd held her in his arms afterward and murmured to her in an unfamiliar language. It occurred to her that for the first time since Mark, she would be willing to welcome a man back into her bed.

"Hey, Thea, where've you been? I was trying to call you."

Thea nodded at Matt who sat at the head of the large table. He was alone in the room. Thea took the seat next to him and lowered her voice.

"It was my night off. Things got a little complicated and I woke up late."

Matt studied her until she started to shift in her chair.

"What?"

"You tell me. I'm no expert but I think I can tell when a woman has been well-fucked. There's a certain look in her eyes."

Thea felt her cheeks heat. "It's none of your business."

Matt sat back. "Yeah, right. It's just a coincidence then that a certain red-haired Valhallan male was out all night as well?"

Thea glanced over her shoulder as the Earth security team began to fill the room. "If you promise not to tell anyone, I'll fill you in later."

He winked at her. "Cross my heart and hope to die. If he made you look this happy, he deserves my thanks."

In a desperate attempt to change the subject, Thea asked, "Do you have any idea what this meeting is about?"

"None at all, you? Surely, you must be getting the best information these days."

Thea bared her teeth at him and he laughed. His expression sobered as the Valhallans filed into the room, their expressions grim. Thea tried to catch Sven's eye but his attention remained on the queen as he helped her into her seat.

Matt inclined his head respectfully to the king. "It is always a pleasure to meet with you, Sire. What can I do for you?"

"Firstly, we wish to speak to you and Ms. Cooper alone."

Matt nodded at the other members of his team who got up and left. After the door closed behind the last of them, the king glanced at the queen who nodded.

"We have been warned that a certain entertainment show, The *Daily Scream* with Mick Jarvis, plans on running an exposé piece about the queen and her bodyguards."

Thea frowned. "We have received no information about this and we certainly wouldn't have sanctioned any release of information to that particular show."

"That's what I thought." The king's hard gaze swept over them. "We intend to cooperate with you fully to ensure that this invasion into our privacy is avoided."

Matt sat forward. "Of course, Sire, we'd be happy to help." He hesitated, "What exactly is Mick Jarvis proposing to show?"

Sven leaned forward and laid a series of blurred still-images on the table. "This is what we received."

Matt and Thea both picked one up. Thea tried to make out the indistinct black and white images.

"It looks like a pile of bodies."

"It is." Matt passed Thea the piece of paper he held. It was a color version of the same scene. Thea's stomach clenched as she focused on a familiar shock of dark red hair. She tried to keep her voice from trembling.

"Well, one of the guys looks like Mr. Magnusson."

"You are correct, Ms. Cooper." The queen answered, her worried gaze flicked between Sven who sat in stony silence beside her, to Thea and Matt. "And the others would be Harlan, Bron and…me."

Thea couldn't help but stare at the king who looked remarkably calm. He met her gaze and smiled.

"I can see that you believe I have been…what is that charming Earth expression? Ah, yes, cuckolded."

Matt gathered up the papers and cleared his throat. "With all due respect, Sire, that is a reasonable assumption to make."

The king shrugged. "Our customs are different on Valhalla. When I am not able to pleasure the queen, I rely on my wife's servers to keep her satisfied and ready to mate with me on my return."

"Ah, I see."

Thea looked down at her hands, her fingers were shaking. The blurred image of Sven's red hair against the pale skin of the queen's breast as he suckled her had burned itself into her brain. He'd lied to her. She wasn't stupid, his allegiance to the queen was far more important to him than anything he might feel for her. She'd been used. The king had come back to claim his wife and Sven had obviously decided he needed an outlet for his sexual energy. And Thea had been all too eager to oblige. Exactly why had she gotten involved with someone she had to work with again?

She realized Matt was speaking and gathered her shattered attention.

"What exactly do you want us to do, Sire?"

"I would prefer that these pictures or any film footage not be released to the public. They are likely to be misunderstood and I will not have my queen's reputation smeared on her own planet."

There was an underlying note of steel in the king's politely worded request that made Matt sit up straight.

"Of course, I'll talk to the President and our lawyers. As a welcome ambassador to our planet, you will be afforded all the protection our laws can supply."

The king inclined his head. "I appreciate that. If you need our help, please liaise with Sven." He stood up and drew the queen to her feet. "We will be with our son, awaiting your report."

Matt and Thea stood up as the king and queen made their exit. Sven hung back, his gaze fixed on Thea. She deliberately avoided his eyes and turned to Matt.

"I'll see you later. I have some security details to review regarding the positioning of the camera that took those photos. Let me know if there are any developments."

Sven caught her arm as she rushed past him.

"Thea…"

She pulled out of his grasp. "Excuse me, Mr. Magnusson, but I have a lot of work to do. Perhaps you'd be better off consoling your queen?"

His expression darkened. "I wish to speak with you, not the queen. Why do you think I asked if you could sit in on that meeting? I wanted you to hear the truth. The queen already understands what is going on. You don't."

She gave him her best death-ray glare. "I think I do. You aren't the first man I've dated who's turned out to be a two-timing rat bastard."

She managed to get into the hallway and keep going until she reached the sanctuary of her office. Ten seconds later, Sven barged in and shut the door with a resounding crash behind him.

"Thea, you do not understand. "

"It's Ms. Cooper, to you."

He ignored her and advanced two steps closer until she was pressed up against her desk. He placed his hands flat on the surface, caging her between them.

"How can you try to distance yourself from me after the night we shared? You honored me with your body, you gave me a taste of paradise."

"Wow, are you saying I'm a better lay than the queen? Thanks."

His jaw tightened. "My relationship with the queen is not the same."

"Oh right, its part of your job description isn't it? I forgot. Fuck the queen when the king's away."

"It is not like that."

"Can you honestly say that you haven't been with her? You told me that you'd only had sex with one woman, ever! Or was that another lie?"

He took a deep shuddering breath. "Thea, the queen has nothing to do with how I feel about you. With you, it is different. It is what I want, not what my culture dictates."

Tears pricked at the corner of her eyes. He'd completely avoided answering the question. She managed a brittle laugh.

"Poor little Sven. Don't worry about it. We're done anyway."

He held her gaze. "What do you mean?"

"It was just business."

Sven went still.

"Matt asked me to get close to you so that I could give him better information. He knows I never sleep with any man more than once."

"You lie."

The low menacing rumble of Sven's voice made Thea tighten her grip on the edge of the table.

"Ask Matt. He'll tell you. So we're even. Sleeping with you was just part of my job description too."

He took a step back, his expression lethal.

"Do you fuck every male your boss asks you to?"

"Do you fuck every female the king asks you to?"

Sven closed his eyes. "I was going to ask you to come back to Valhalla and be my one true mate, but it seems I was deceived." He bowed. "I beg your pardon."

Thea could only watch as he turned and walked away from her, closing the door with a firm click behind him. She felt the hot sting of tears on her cheeks and let them fall as she continued to stare into the nothingness her love life had suddenly become.

"We've managed to prevent Mick Jarvis from using the footage tonight, but, as the queen probably knows, these things have a way of leaking out. This is what we propose."

Sven let out his breath as Matt Logan looked expectantly at the king. The Valhallans were so large they made Matt's office feel as small as the queen's closet. And where was Thea? Sven's gut clenched as he registered her absence.

"I am glad to hear you have been successful." Marcus inclined his head. "My Queen and I appreciate your efforts. What can we do to help you in return?"

"We're going to move the photo shoot with *Greetings*! magazine forward to this afternoon and make sure the article that accompanies the photos makes the um, slightly more ambivalent sexual customs on Valhalla clearer to the public, without spelling them out, of course." Matt tugged at his tie. "Hopefully that will lessen the impact of any photos that are released illegally."

"That seems like a workable plan."

Matt nodded. "I'm glad you think so. The other thing we believe might be beneficial is to speed up your departure to Valhalla. We had planned to leave in two weeks but we believe we might be able to make it in less than one."

The king frowned. "We do not wish to look as if we are running away. We are not ashamed of our planet's customs."

"I understand that, Sire."

"Then I agree."

Sven hardly noticed the relief on Matt Logan's face as he turned away from the king. He moved swiftly toward the door and blocked Matt's exit.

"Where is Ms. Cooper?"

"Nowhere she wants you to find her, buddy."

The hostility in Matt's voice made Sven narrow his eyes. Matt moved past him forcing Sven to catch him up in the hallway.

"I repeat. Where is she?"

"Trust me, you don't want to know. You're not her favorite person at the moment."

"And what does this have to do with you? Are you her messenger boy?"

"Nope, I'm her friend and I'm not prepared to see another selfish jerk trample her feelings into the ground. Christ, I'd just got her to dip her toe into dating again after Mark and you turn up and set her back 5 freaking years."

Who was Mark? A wave of raw jealousy shuddered through Sven. Oblivious to the people around him, he grabbed Matt by the shirt.

"I am losing patience. Where is she?"

Matt met his threatening glare head on. "Out checking the perimeter fence, you dickhead, but I wouldn't go chasing after her. She'll probably shoot you on sight."

"I'll take my chances."

Sven shoved Matt against the wall and headed down the stairs. Thea had avoided him all morning. He wasn't prepared to give her too many chances to escape him again.

"Sven."

He kept walking until he reached the garden, aware that someone was following him but too intent on his quest to care.

"Sven, stop."

He came to a halt, half-turned and realized the king was behind him.

"Sire?"

"Leave Ms. Cooper be."

Sven took a slow breath. "Sire, I can't do that."

"You must."

"I...owe her an explanation. She thinks I have been intimate with the queen."

The king half-smiled. "You have."

"Sire, I have only acted on your orders and in accordance with my vows to serve your consort."

The king folded his arms across his massive chest. "Then it is my fault? You told me you were honored to serve my queen. Have you not enjoyed your duties?"

"That is not what I meant. I hold the queen in high regard."

Sven looked anywhere but at the king. How in Odin's name had he become embroiled in such a personal conversation? His feelings for Thea were far too raw to be shared. The king reached him and lightly touched his shoulder.

"Sven, you will have plenty of time to sort things out with Ms. Cooper after we reach Valhalla. Let her calm down. When she sees how we live, she might be more amenable to listening to you."

"She is hardly likely to come to Valhalla now, is she?"

"She will if the queen and I insist."

Sven finally met the king's gaze. "Thank you, Sire."

Marcus punched him hard on the shoulder. "Thank the queen. She has taught me a lot about how to deal with Earth females over the last year."

Thea glanced at the clock. Thank god the day was almost over. She'd had to endure three hours of watching the king and the Valhallan court pose for *Greetings!* magazine. The only thing that had raised her level of misery was that Sven hadn't managed to crack a smile once, even after the photographer had insisted. How many cheesy shots of the king and queen cooing over their son could a planet want to see? Thousands, if the *Greetings*! staff were to be believed.

"Happy family, my foot," Thea muttered. No wonder everyone was so happy when they got all the sex they wanted whenever they wanted it. And to think she'd felt bad for Sven when he'd suggested he'd only known one other woman in his life. As far as he was concerned, he'd simply had a scheduling problem trying to do both women at the same time.

She put away her files and shut off her communication system. At least she hadn't suggested they get together again. Her pride couldn't have taken another blow. A quick work-out in the gym should relieve some of the stress she'd accumulated throughout the day and stretch the soreness out of her overused muscles. Sven hadn't bothered to come and find her since their initial confrontation in her office. Part of her had hoped he would…

"Traitor." Thea admonished her own body as her hormones leaped to attention, completely failing to understand why she wasn't going to be leaping into the sack with Sven every night. She sure hoped the gym was deserted.

She was granted her wish and soon settled into her usual exercise routine. After failing to reach any of her personal bests, a grueling stint on the treadmill seemed the only suitable way to end her less than perfect day.

When the gym door opened, she glanced up, and saw Harlan, one of the other Valhallan bodyguards. Although he was tall, he wasn't quite as broad as Sven. His hair was black and long, drawn away from the high cheekbones of his face. His frame was muscular without the slight stockiness of Sven's and his legs seemed to go on forever. She frowned at him. Why was she even bothering to compare him to Sven? Sven was *so* not her ideal man.

Harlan bowed, his long black braid sliding over his shoulder. "May I join you, my lady?"

"It's a free country."

He paused by the abs machine. "I do not understand what that has to do with my working out alongside you."

"I mean, the gym is open for all, so be my guest."

Harlan stripped down to his shorts and headed for the machine beside her. He fiddled with the controls and set a fast jogging pace. To Thea's annoyance, unlike her, he didn't even break into a sweat or start to breathe harder. She stared straight ahead of her and kept jogging until her legs felt like lead.

"Did you enjoy your mating with Sven?"

Thea stopped abruptly and just remembered to turn off the machine before she fell flat on her ass. "Wow, you're very direct, aren't you?"

He raised his eyebrows. "I have offended you?"

"Oh no, that's what we do here on Earth, we always discuss our love lives with the first person who asks for details."

"I have offended you. Forgive me. We were all so delighted when Sven spent the night with you."

Thea drew in a shaky breath. "Oh great. Did he go into all the gory details and how did the queen feel about that?"

Harlan smiled. "You are more polite than your mate. Sven threatened to beat me to a pulp when I asked him."

"He didn't tell you anything?"

Harlan got off the treadmill, his skin gleaming with sweat. "He told me to mind my own business, much as you have done."

Thea held his gaze. "I'm not his mate."

"He seems to think you are."

"One night does not a relationship or a mating make."

"Maybe that is true on Earth. But one night is enough for a male from my planet to make up his mind."

Thea crossed her arms over her chest. "From what I've heard, any male who manages to find a female on your planet is bound to fall instantly in love with her."

"That is not true."

"Are you sure? Females are so rare, any man who catches one would probably be prepared to do or say anything to keep her."

Harlan smiled. "Valhallan males are not stupid. A woman who is unhappy does not make a good mate or a life partner. Why would any man want that?"

"So you all sit around waiting for that perfect person?"

"In an ideal world, yes of course. There are males on our planet who are prepared to risk anything to keep a female, but they will be in a minority now that the fertility problems have been resolved."

Thea grabbed her towel. "So it's all good then. Sven can go home and find himself someone new. If the queen's okay with that, of course."

"The queen wishes her servers to be happy."

Thea turned abruptly away from Harlan and closed her eyes. There was that word again, happy. The Valhallans were so full of it. She swung back around and glared at Harlan.

"The queen gets to have her cake and eat it."

Harlan looked puzzled. "And what is wrong with eating cake?"

"I mean, she wins either way. She has the king and all of you guys eating out of her hand, giving her sex whenever she wants it…" Thea's voice trailed away as she imagined the queen writhing between all those strong sweaty male bodies.

"The queen is an amazing woman."

"I bet she is. I don't know how she manages you all."

Harlan bent to pick up his clothes. "Ms. Cooper, are you jealous?"

"Of a woman who can satisfy four men? Of course not."

Harlan came toward her, his expression amused. He used his white T-shirt to rub at the sweat on his muscled chest. "You do not understand our ways. Perhaps you should ask Sven or the queen to explain matters to you more clearly."

Thea clutched at her towel as he towered over her. He was so close that she could see his pupils had shards of silver buried in the gray.

"I understand everything perfectly, thank you."

"Nay, you don't." Harlan touched her cheek, his fingers soft. "Talk to Sven again."

Thea stepped back. "Don't tell me what to do."

"It was merely a suggestion." Harlan bowed and walked back toward the door. "Sven is a proud stubborn man and I fear that unless you approach him, he will simply turn his back on his chance of happiness."

Thea shook her head. "Don't try to make me feel bad. He's the one who's fooling around with two women, not me."

"Sven is no fool."

"No, I suppose you're right." Thea walked across to the locker room door, pausing before she opened it. "He's probably worked out that he's been found out by now. Will the queen dump him as well?"

"Sven has made vows to the queen."

"She's *married* to him?"

Harlan laughed out loud. "Nay, all her servers made sacred vows to the king to serve the queen."

"The king sure is relaxed about this." Thea attempted a sneer. "And he looks like such an Alpha male. I wouldn't have thought sharing was his thing."

"Exactly."

"What the hell is that supposed to mean?"

"The king doesn't share."

Briefly Thea closed her eyes. "Harlan, if you have something to say, just spit it out."

"I don't spit."

"Tell me!"

"Ms. Cooper, it is not my place to interfere between you and your mate. Ask Sven."

With a last glare, Thea pushed the door into the locker room and went through. Just what she needed. Another man with a body to die for and a strange take on the realities of life. Were all Valhallan males like this? Determined to speak in riddles? She headed for the shower hoping the water would clear her head and maybe hide the tears she was still aching to shed.

She almost went into reverse when she emerged from the locker room and found Matt leaning up against the opposite wall. He fell into step beside her.

"I know this isn't a good time, but I need to talk to you."

Thea glanced at him. He wasn't smiling and his tone was all business.

"I was about to go home, can't it wait until the morning?"

"No."

Matt grabbed her arm and maneuvered her into a vacant office. It smelled of burned toast and old coffee. He sat on the edge of the desk and stared at her.

"What's the worst piece of news I could give you right now?"

"Um, Mick Jarvis has got his hands on a sex tape of me and Sven?"

Matt paused and raised his eyebrows. "He was that good?"

"Shut up."

"How about this, then. The Valhallans have requested that you accompany the initial return party back to their planet."

"No way am I doing that." Thea dropped her bag to the floor. "Don't they know what happened?"

"They do, but the queen insists she wants a female bodyguard to accompany her."

"You told them I wouldn't do it, right?"

"I tried but…"

"It doesn't have to be me, does it?"

Matt shrugged. "We'd like it to be you."

Thea kicked the door shut with the heel of her shoe. "When you say, 'we' are you speaking for your multiple personalities or for the government?"

"The government. It would take too long to bring another female bodyguard up to speed before the Valhallans leave, and you have developed a good relationship with the queen and the rest of them."

Thea leaned up against the door. "Matt, I don't want this. I really don't want to be trapped with Sven Magnusson for five minutes, let alone on a long space journey to the edge of our galaxy."

"We need to play nice with them. We still need their land for future colonization."

"So you're prepared to sacrifice what I want for the good of the government?" His implacable expression didn't change. "I bet you didn't even stand up for me. I thought you were my friend."

Matt got up from the table. "I am your friend but I want to succeed in my career as well. Can't you understand that?"

Thea picked up her bag. "There's a hell of a lot I'm not understanding at the moment but you putting your career ahead of our friendship? That sounds way too familiar."

"I'm not like Mark, Thea."

She swallowed the lump in her throat. "No, you're not. I always knew he might leave me, but I figured we were friends to the end."

"Shit, Thea..."

She shouldered her gym bag and gave him a smile.

"No worries. I'll think over what you've just told me tonight and decide whether it's worth resigning over."

Mat stared down at his hands. "The government won't accept your resignation, you know that."

"I'll still think about it. This isn't the only planet in the solar system."

"You can't always run away from stuff."

"I'm not running."

Matt took a hasty step toward her. "Yeah, you are. You did it over Mark and hey, you're doing it again over Sven. Much easier to blame me and the government for your mess ups than take responsibility and deal with them yourself."

A hot shiver of rage licked at Thea's stomach. "I am sick to death of everyone telling me how to run my life!"

"How about you stand up for yourself and fight for what you want then?"

She glared at him. "You don't know what I want."

"Neither do you."

"I want to be left alone."

"Oh yeah, that's right, because if you're alone you don't have to risk anything, do you? And if you don't think you're worth sticking around for, how the hell is any guy supposed to believe it?"

"Matt..."

Thea flung open the door and marched away as fast as she could. The exit door loomed in front of her and she just managed to fumble her way out before the tears returned. Okay, her definition of the worst day ever was now today. She wasn't convinced that a gallon of her favorite ice cream would even make a dent in how awful she felt.

She climbed into her vehicle and turned the music up loud. How dare Matt turn everything around and make her the bad guy? She was the one who'd been hurt and betrayed wasn't she? Perhaps the cosmos were trying to tell her something. Stay away from males. She wiped her eyes and stared defiantly out at the busy traffic on the freeway. All those guys could go to hell. She was quite capable of surviving without any of them.

Chapter Seven

ℬ

"We have entered orbit around Planet Valhalla. Please feel free to move around the ship."

The calm female voice of the ship's guidance systems echoed around the passenger recovery bay. Thea grimaced as she climbed out of the stasis capsule and rubbed her dry eyes. She'd been warned that when she was allowed out of the claustrophobic plastic pod her body would be stiff as a board. With a groan, she started on the series of warm up exercises she used when she was at the gym.

While touching her toes she got a close up view of a pair of big bare feet. She straightened too quickly and bumped into Sven's chest. He caught her elbow to steady her and she felt her cheeks heat. He wore a pair of regulation yellow space pants, slung way too low on his hips and nothing else except two gold armbands.

"Are you all right, Ms. Cooper?"

God, he smelled so good, so warm and welcoming. She swayed toward him and immediately pulled her arm free.

"I'm fine. What do you want?"

He met her gaze, his brown eyes as shuttered as her own. "It's my job to make sure everyone comes out of stasis. I'm just checking on your general wellbeing."

"My well-being is just fine and dandy thanks. Even better if you'd leave me alone."

He sighed. "Thea…"

She raised her chin to stare right into his eyes. "I thought we'd agreed it would be Ms. Cooper from now on?"

"We haven't agreed anything." She tried to move past him and he frowned. "By Thor's blood, will you not even speak to me?"

"I'll speak to you when it is relevant to the mission. That's it, Mr. Magnusson."

He caught her elbow and yanked her against his chest. She could feel the heavy beat of his heart, the tension humming through his large frame.

"We're on my planet now, my lady. The rules have changed. You won't be able to avoid me so easily."

She watched his luscious mouth form the words, heard the subtle threat behind them and still wanted to kiss him more than she wanted to breathe. Deliberately she stood on his toes. He winced but didn't release her.

"Let me go, Mr. Magnusson or my next target will be your family jewels."

"I will if you agree to talk to me tomorrow."

His tone was inflexible, his face as hard as moonstone.

"All right."

He stepped back and bowed. "Thank you my lady."

She moved past him, found her way to one of the observation windows and looked out at the planet they orbited. She gasped. It really was purple. She'd seen the images but nothing had prepared her for the glinting shifting many-hued reality of the planet's surface.

"It's beautiful."

"Aye, my lady, it is."

"Go *away*, Mr. Magnusson."

There was an amused chuckle. She jumped as the king's reflection appeared alongside her own. He nodded.

"We are grateful for your planet's help in restoring ours." He held her gaze, his golden eyes full of emotion. "At times, I thought I would never see it again, let alone find it restored and free of pollution."

Thea cleared her throat. "I'm pleased that you are pleased, Sire."

"I give thanks daily to our gods that my queen appeared to save my planet and me."

Thea stared at his massive chest and neck, noticed a fading bruise on his throat. His love and respect for the queen was obvious in everything he did. How could he countenance her sleeping with other men?

"The queen is a lucky woman, Sire."

He laughed, the low sound almost a purr of satisfaction. "Nay, I am the lucky one. She brings me great joy with her presence and her body. She has given me a son."

Thea frowned. Was that it? Was the king prepared to give the queen anything she desired simply because she had given him a son? She knew how important children were to the Valhallans. His expression sobered.

"Is something wrong, Ms. Cooper?"

"No, Sire, I'm just trying to imagine how it would feel to be loved like that."

The king smoothed a hand over his chest and then down to his groin. Thea followed the movement of his hand and then realized he was half-erect. She quickly raised her eyes to his smiling face.

"From what I have heard, Ms. Cooper, Sven would be more than happy to show you."

"Mr. Magnusson and I are merely fellow workers."

"Is that so?" the king smiled. "Then you will surely appreciate his company while you are on my planet. I have assigned him to be your personal escort."

Thea gaped at the king, who nodded and turned away. What was wrong with everyone? Were they all determined to push her and Sven together? She headed for the shower, ignoring Harlan and Bron who smiled and bowed to her. She wasn't about to stop and chat with any more Valhallan males determined to set her straight about Sven and send her back into his arms.

The female shower was already operating. Thea sighed as she stepped under the hot stream of water.

"Ms. Cooper. How was your journey?"

Thea opened her eyes and found the queen emerging through the steam, her skin flushed, her long dark hair already washed and hanging down her back. Oh crap, this was *so* not who she wanted to talk to right now.

"The journey was fine thanks." Thea made an awkward gesture. "Do you want to shower alone, Your Highness?"

The queen winced. "Oh jeez, please call me Douglass. We only use titles when we're in public and I'm not even comfortable with that yet. I'm so glad you agreed to come with us. Sometimes I get a bit sick of all the testosterone surrounding me."

Thea flashed an uneasy smile. There were quite a few answers to that statement, none of which were diplomatic and several of which would probably get her ass fired. For some reason she had no desire to be stranded in space, subject to Valhallan law and without a ticket home. God knows what the punishment would be for calling the queen a bitch and getting into a cat fight.

"Is there something, wrong?"

"Oh no, Your Highness, I mean Douglass, and please call me Thea."

"Thank you, Thea, I appreciate it." The queen sighed. "Sometimes I miss hanging with my girlfriends on Earth. Men just don't understand some stuff do they?"

"But they have some uses."

Douglass smiled dreamily. "They sure do. Marcus will be all over me the moment I step out of this shower."

Remembering the king's state of arousal, Thea didn't doubt it. *And what about Sven and the others? When do they get a turn?* Thea stared hard at the wall, desperate not to say the words out loud.

"Sven is very taken with you, Thea."

Thea continued to wash her hair and hoped the queen would think she hadn't heard that last comment. What the hell was she supposed to say? What was the queen going to do next, discuss Sven's prowess in bed?

Douglass sighed. "I'm sorry. It's none of my business, I know. It's just that I care for Sven and I was kind of hoping you'd be the right woman for him. If you feel like talking to me, you know where I am."

Thea kept her head under the water until she heard the queen walk away. It seemed everyone liked Sven except her. Was she missing something important or was it simply that her personal standards were so different from the Valhallans and their new queen? Surely Douglass would understand that Thea didn't want to share her man? Too tired to think anymore, Thea finished her shower, dressed in the shapeless yellow spacesuit and looked forward to her first real glimpse of the planet's surface.

Due to the haste of their departure, only five members of the Earth observation team disembarked along with Thea. Two of them were hand-picked members of the press; the other three represented the Planetary Health Organization and the government. Thea wasn't quite sure what her role was, despite the fact that the Valhallans had asked for her input on security matters and insisted she was needed to guard the queen.

As she walked toward the space terminal, Thea stopped and inhaled the fragrant scent of flowers and spices. The planets two suns were setting in an azure sky and the desert sand glimmered and shifted around her like the sea. A soft breeze lowered the high temperature to a bearable level. Groves of green trees covered with thick blossoms stretched into the distance, nestling against the darkness of the mountains that rose in the west.

"By Thor, it is good to be home." Thea glanced up and saw Sven's reverent expression. He studied the desert and the twinkling lights of the space port. "I thought I would never see it again."

She stopped looking at him, almost overwhelmed by the gruffness of his voice. His obvious emotion reminded her of the way he'd looked down at her when they'd made love. She slowed her pace, let him overtake her and reach the scattered buildings first. The perfumed air felt heavy as it closed over her skin.

"My lady?"

She realized Sven waited at the door for her. He bowed and indicated the large white flower in his hands.

"On my planet, it is customary to welcome visitors with a flower from the *ozan* tree. Will you accept this from me?"

She realized that the king, the queen and all the Earth visitors were waiting to see what she did. She was a grown-up. She didn't have to air her private grievances with Sven in public. With a smile she accepted the flower.

"Thank you. It's beautiful."

Sven tucked it behind her left ear and then knelt before her.

"I am honored, my lady."

The heavy fragrance filled her senses and she closed her eyes to savor it. After a moment, her eyes snapped open. She looked down at Sven's bent head, tried to resist the urge to lick the delicious shadowed curve where his neck met his shoulders.

"Hey, how come I'm the only one who got a flower?"

Sven got to his feet, and guessed from Thea's tone that she'd registered the smile of pure male satisfaction on his face.

"Because you are the only unattached female."

Her eyes flashed and her fingers moved toward the flower. He caught them in his own. The potent smell of the petals mingled with her familiar female scent and made him rock hard. The emotions he'd experienced on returning home were still far too close to the surface for him to accept her dismissal lightly.

"Please," he murmured. "Do not shame me in front of my people. You look beautiful. Accept this gift."

She let out her breath and he reluctantly released her hand. Her sudden smile was breathtaking.

"Thank you for honoring me. The flower is lovely."

He bowed low, relief flooding through him at her gracious words. "Of course, my lady." He gestured to the front of the space port. "Our transport is outside."

She strode off without him. He grunted when she came to a complete stop and bumped up against his chest.

"What the hell is that?" she whispered.

"Our transport."

"That big green chicken?"

"It is a *wulfrun*.

"It is a disaster. It looks like a giant chicken mated with a dragon."

The *wulfrun* looked up as if he was offended and blew hot steam out of its nose. Thea moved closer to Sven who smiled and greeted the *wulfrun* in his own language.

"Hvordan har de det?"

He reached out a hand to stroke the beast's long neck. The *wulfrun* bowed its head and clawed at the ground.

"What did you say to it?"

"I just asked him how he was."

Sven nodded his thanks as one of the grooms threw a blanket over the animal's back and handed him the reins. He glanced back at Thea as he pulled himself up on top.

"Give me your hand."

She reacted automatically, placing her palm into his. With a grin, he leaned down, slid his hand down to her elbow and swung her up in front of him. The second her butt hit the blanket, she started to struggle.

"I'm not sitting on this thing with you."

Sven wrapped his arm around her waist.

"You wish to ride alone or be left behind?" He gestured at the space port. "As you can see, we are the only people left."

She turned to look at him. He could've sworn there were tears in her eyes.

"Sometimes I think I hate you, Sven Magnusson."

He curved his arm around her more securely, drawing her back toward his groin. She fitted against him so well and yet her words hurt more than he could have believed possible.

"I regret, I cannot say the same, my lady."

She sniffed loudly and braced one of her hands on his thigh, the other rested on his hand around her waist. He clicked his teeth to the *wulfrun* and her grip tightened.

"Are you sure these things are safe?"

"If you trust me, then yes."

"Trust *you*?"

Sven let out a ragged breath. "My lady, I am weary of this fighting. Why don't you just sit back and enjoy the scenery?"

He tensed as she slowly turned her head to stare at him.

"You're right. I'm in no shape to keep this up tonight and it sure is beautiful out here. I'll be polite, okay?"

Sven frowned. He didn't want her being polite. He wanted her naked and astride him, begging to be fucked. His cock stirred and lengthened, pushed eagerly at the thin yellow fabric of his pants and branded Thea's spine. He knew exactly when she became aware of it because she tried to move away. He kept her close, her arm firm around her waist.

"Dammit, Sven. That's not quite the scenery I was hoping to sit back and enjoy."

"I am a man, not a statue. I cannot stop my cock from still wanting you." Greatly daring, Sven kissed the top of her head. "Just touching you makes me hard. I remember the sounds of ecstasy you made when I suckled your breasts and slid my cock deep into your wet welcoming channel."

"I thought you said we didn't need to talk?"

She moved restlessly against him and he bit back a groan. He slid his hand lower until the tips of his fingers brushed her mound.

"Is it the same for you, my lady? Do you still think about making love with me?" The scent of her arousal rose up and he inhaled greedily. "If I slid my fingers deep inside you now, would you be wet for me?"

A shout ahead, made him look reluctantly back up at the terrain. The lights of the main palace were clearly visible on the horizon. The *wulfrun* lifted his head and increased his speed, keen to get back to his stable. Thea gasped and dug her nails into his hand.

Sven sat deeper and allowed his hips to move into the new faster rhythm, aware that his shaft rubbed against Thea's ass with every forward movement. By the time they reached the outer wall of the palace, he was fighting the urge to come with every tortured breath.

As soon as the *wulfrun* stopped, Thea threw herself out of his arms and dropped to the ground. Sven stayed where he was, unable to move until his cock allowed him to. A groom ran to hold the *wulfrun*'s head and Sven finally managed to dismount. To his surprise, Thea waited for him. His anticipation rose. Perhaps she realized she wanted him after all. He strolled toward her, making no effort to hide the extent of his arousal.

"Is there something I can do for you, my lady?"

"No, I'm ...fine...just fine."

She stared at his rock-hard shaft and licked her lips as if remembering how he tasted. Unable to deny the wave of frustrated lust powering through him, he maneuvered her backward until she was up against the stable wall. Without waiting for permission, he lowered his mouth and slid his tongue between her opened lips. He ravaged her mouth the way he wanted to penetrate her—rough, hard and fast, taking no prisoners, allowing her no choice but to accept him.

His hand fisted in her hair as she kissed him back and he groaned.

"Thea..."

He choked as she grabbed his balls and squeezed tight. He slowly straightened until he could see her determined face.

"Sven, you are driving me crazy." She gripped him harder. "If you don't back off right now, I'm going to twist your fine assets until you scream."

He nodded and held his hands high, palms open.

"Backing off, my lady."

"Okay, then."

She looked down at her hand and Sven sighed as she slowly released him. Her thumb brushed his shaft and his cock jerked. He growled helplessly as his cum erupted, soaking her hand and the front of his pants.

"Oh dear." She wiped her fingers on her pants. "Sorry about that."

Sven rubbed the wet patch on his pants and cupped himself. His breathing was uneven, his body shaking and out of control from this smallest of encounters with the woman he craved. He gulped in some of the perfumed night air and then bowed.

"May I show you to your quarters? We have allocated you a suite near the queen."

Thea allowed Sven to walk into the palace ahead of her. The walls were a soft cream color and the floors were tiled with red and blue mosaics and other intricate patterns. Soft drapes covered the open windows, allowing the balmy heat from the desert to freshen the hallways and the rooms opening off them. She looked up as they passed through yet another gateway and realized that at its center, the palace was several stories high and ringed by a series of gated courtyards. It reminded her of a circular maze.

As she walked, she rubbed her fingers against her thigh. God, who would've thought Sven, would react like that to her touch? The thought that he hadn't been able to stop himself from coming was strangely erotic. He walked ahead of her, his stride long and confident, his pants so low on his hips now that she could see the dimples at the top of his ass. She'd resorted to threats to stop herself from throwing her body into his arms and begging him to make love to her.

She winced. What was wrong with her? Why did she insist on lusting after men who were no good for her? Perhaps Matt had a point and she needed to learn to love herself first.

"Your chamber is here, my lady."

Sven opened an ornate door and Thea stepped past him into a bedroom straight from the Arabian nights. A large bed, draped in soft netting dominated the room, thick patterned rugs covered the pink marble floor and the large windows looked out toward the purple desert.

"It is beautiful. Please thank the queen and king for me."

"Aye, I will."

Sven remained at the door, arms crossed over his chest, head bowed. Soft candlelight illuminated his gold armbands and exposed the lines of strain on his face. Thea managed a smile.

"Will I see you in the morning?"

He bowed. "We break our fast at daybreak. The queen will send a servant to make sure you are up."

"Well, say thanks to her when you kiss her goodnight."

Thea tensed as Sven grabbed the doorframe with one massive hand and squeezed so hard the wood groaned.

"I am not on duty, tonight. Sleep well, my lady."

He turned and left, shutting the door quietly behind him. Thea stared at the gold and white panels. Sven was in the wrong, wasn't he? So why did she suddenly feel like the bad guy?

God, what a fabulous dream…

Thea moaned and undulated her hips against the pressure of Sven's mouth on her clit. This dream was so good; she was going to have to make herself come. With a sigh, she let her hand drift down between her legs and encounter thick, silky hair. Either she'd changed into a werewolf during the night or this wasn't a dream.

With a shriek, Thea sat up, dislodging the bare-chested man between her legs. He smiled at her.

"Good morning, my lady."

"What the hell do you think you're doing?" She grabbed the silk sheet and held it to her breasts.

The man looked puzzled. "Waking you up?"

"I have an alarm clock for that! Not…" Thea waved at his mouth and he licked his lips.

"The queen sent me to serve you. It is a great honor to be chosen. My name is Woden, after the god of war, but some people called me Den."

His eyes were pale blue and his hair was dark brown and almost to his shoulders. Like all the Valhallan men he was tall and broad with muscles to die for. He wore nothing but a thin white strip of silk at his groin which did little to conceal or contain the extent of his erection.

"Don't tell me. All the women on Valhalla get woken up like this."

"If they are not with their mate, then yes. Is it not the same on your planet?" Woden stroked her ankle. "Would you like me to finish? You didn't climax."

"I would like you to leave so that I can get up and have a shower."

He moved off the bed and held out his hand. "There is no need for me to leave. I am here to help you."

"Woden, I am quite capable of getting up by myself."

He stepped back, his hand falling to his side. "I have offended you."

Thea got off the bed, still holding the sheet to her breasts. "No, you haven't. It's just that this isn't the way I'm used to starting my day."

"The males on your planet do not pleasure you in the morning?"

"Not every day."

Woden frowned. "Why not?"

Thea edged toward the bathroom she had discovered the previous night. "Because they have to get to work."

"But surely they make time to attend to your needs?"

"Um, no. If anything, it's usually the other way round."

"They expect you to service them?" Woden paused to pick up the trailing end of Thea's sheet and handed it to her. He glanced down at his cock. "A male wouldn't last long on this planet if he was that selfish."

While he talked, Thea busied herself in the bathroom, located the shower and let the sheet fall to the floor. With a sigh, she closed her eyes and stepped under the water. Woden's erect cock brushed her hip as he followed her right in.

"I thought I told you I could take care of this myself?"

"But you don't have to." He smoothed his well-soaped hands down her flanks and then up over her breasts. Her nipples peaked in response and he murmured his approval.

"Your breasts are beautiful, my lady, your nipples hardened in my mouth when I suckled you this morning."

God, why hadn't she woken up when he did that? She moved restlessly against him as he continued to soap her body. This wasn't right but it was so difficult to stop him without hurting his feelings.

"Relax, my lady. I just wish to help you."

She sighed, leaned back against his chest and felt the thick press of his cock. Her government had stressed the need to respond appropriately to the local customs on Valhalla. Was this an appropriate reaction or not? Woden's fingers slipped between her thighs, bringing the ache back he'd created earlier. He penetrated her with two fingers, used the rest to soap her folds and rub her clit. She came fast and hard, her hips jerking forward as he bit down on the nape of her neck. God, she wished it had been Sven.

"You are beautiful when you come. I am honored to have served you."

He continued to wash her, falling to his knees and licking at her already swollen clit. She touched the top of his sleek wet head. Her voice sounded off-key.

"Don't we need to go?"

He smiled up at her. "If you permit, I'll bring you to your pleasure once more and then prepare your clothing."

Thea smiled weakly as he sucked her clit into his mouth.

"Well, okay, then, but don't take too long about it."

Woden insisted on escorting Thea to the queen's suite where breakfast was being held. He'd added soft white pants to his attire which did little to hide his nakedness or his half-erect cock. Thea concentrated on walking in front of him, hoping no one would notice his arousal or wonder if she had anything to do with it.

When she entered the hall, all the Valhallan men stood up. The king pulled out a chair for her to his left.

"Ms. Cooper. I hope you slept well and that Woden satisfied your needs this morning."

Thea felt her cheeks heat as all the men smiled at her. Was it that obvious she'd been sexually serviced or was Woden telling the truth and that was simply what they expected?

"He was very helpful, Sire."

The king nodded at everyone to resume their seats. Beneath the clatter of chairs, the queen leaned across and touched Thea's arm.

"Woden looks very pleased with himself. I hope he didn't offend you."

"No, he was…fine. A bit of a surprise but not offensive at all, no."

"I'm glad to hear that. I'll tell him he may continue to serve you during the duration of your stay."

The queen went to sit back, but Thea grabbed her wrist. "He's going to do that to me every morning?"

The king chuckled as he sat down between them. "Of course. It is considered a woman's right to be pleasured every day." He winked at the queen. "Or several times a day if the woman feels she needs it."

Thea straightened and looked across the table straight into Sven's brown eyes. She thought she'd been briefed on the differences in culture, but nothing had quite prepared her for the reality. In fact, she reckoned the Valhallans had kept quite a lot back. Sven nodded an abrupt greeting and returned his gaze to his plate, chewing stolidly. Did he know what had happened to her that morning? From his lack of expression and desire to talk to her, she guessed he did.

Woden touched her shoulder.

"I will get you some breakfast, my lady."

Thea half-rose from her chair. "It's okay, I can get it myself."

Woden shook his head. "No, my lady. Let me. It is my pleasure."

Thea watched him walk away toward the kitchen. Across the table from her, Sven growled something obscene into his goblet. Thea pasted on a coy smile.

"Are you jealous, Sven?"

Sven looked up at her. "Of what, my lady?"

"Of Woden."

"Why would I be jealous of a man I could beat in a fight with one hand tied behind my back?"

"I don't know about that." She actually managed to simper. "He seemed pretty strong to me."

Sven finished his ale and thumped the goblet down onto the table. "If you no longer care about me, why are you trying to make me angry?"

Thea raised her eyebrows. "I am?"

"Aye, you are, and it's not going to work."

"I wouldn't be so sure about that. You're the one swearing into his beer."

"Perhaps you overrate my attraction to you. Perhaps allowing another man to sexually stimulate you makes you a hypocrite."

Thea drew in a breath. "Now, hang on a minute."

Woden placed a huge platter of food in front of her.

"Here you go, my lady. Would you like me to feed you?"

Thea held Sven's gaze as she ripped into the first thing she picked up off the tray. "No thanks, Woden, I'm good."

The king stood up and everyone fell quiet. He held up his goblet.

"First, I would like to welcome our delegation from Earth and thank them and the rest of the Planetary Health Organization for making our planet safe to live on again."

A chorus of hear-hears and ayes rocked the room.

"This morning, I intend to take you all on a tour of the palace and some of the surrounding countryside. We have made great strides toward making our planet safe, there are still areas where it is better for us to travel in groups, especially if we have females with us." The king glanced down at the queen who frowned back at him. "Despite my wife's reluctance to be restricted in anyway, she understands that sometimes we have to take special measures to ensure the safety of any women in our midst."

The king's hard gaze settled on Thea and he bowed.

"Ms. Cooper, I know you will wish to join the rest of your team exploring the planet surface. We value your input and knowledge on the best way to protect our women. All I ask is that you listen to your guides and take any threat seriously."

"Yes, Sire, I will."

Thea wasn't stupid. She'd read the notes Matt had given her about the major imbalance of Valhallan males to females. Some of the wilder, less educated tribes had refused to move off the planet during the cleanup. They were also the tribes that posed the biggest threat. Damn, she missed Matt. There was no way she would wander off by herself just to prove some feminist point.

The king smiled. "That is good. Sven is an excellent bodyguard."

Silently Thea groaned and glanced at Sven who was watching her, a small smile on his lips. The king's efforts to throw them together were either going to kill or cure her. It would be interesting to see which choice ended up being the most desirable.

Chapter Eight

ℬ

"Wow, it is so beautiful."

Sven smiled as Thea stared out over the purple desert. To his relief, she'd been pleasant and amenable to everyone, including him, during the group outing that day around the palace and the local countryside.

"I'm glad you approve, my lady."

He held the door open for her, as with a last glance over her shoulder, she followed the rest of the party inside. Like the other delegates, she'd asked questions, taken copious notes and obeyed every instruction the king or his bodyguards had given her.

Sven watched her mingle with the others. Despite the fact that she wore the regulation yellow uniform, she was easy to spot, her brown hair tied back from her face, her gray eyes sparkling. He enjoyed her sharp intelligence, the way she picked up on a Valhallan security issue and was able to articulate both her problem with it and a potential solution.

He sighed and leaned back against the wall. She had the enviable ability to appear perfectly happy with everyone else and yet freeze him out with a simple look. He wished he was as capable of hiding his feelings. After watching her with Woden that morning, knowing she'd been pleasured in the most intimate way, he'd failed to hide his irritation and she'd used it to rile him.

"Ms. Cooper is very beautiful, Sven."

As if he'd conjured him, Woden appeared at Sven's shoulder. His gaze was riveted on Thea as she laughed at something Harlan said, her hand placed casually on his arm.

Sven bit back a growl. She'd taken great care not to touch him all day, asking help from everyone but him.

"Sven, do you not agree?"

"Aye, Ms. Cooper is a beautiful woman. But you will do well to remember that she is a visitor here and will be returning to her home planet in a few weeks."

"I know that." Woden sighed. "But perhaps if I please her she will take me home with her?"

Sven glowered down at him. "It is different on Earth. Your services to her would not be appreciated by their males. I believe we make them feel inadequate."

"I'm not surprised. From what Ms. Cooper told me this morning, they are a selfish breed, not worthy of a woman's attention."

Thea turned and saw them together. Her smile died as she reluctantly came toward them.

"Good evening, my lady." Woden bowed.

"Hi, Woden. What's up?"

"Nothing is up, my lady. Unless you mean my cock, which tends to fill out whenever I see you."

Sven groaned. "Woden, she means how are you faring?"

Thea briefly met his gaze, a hint of laughter in her eyes. "Sven's right, but thanks for the information, I'll bear it in mind." She motioned to Sven. "Is this a good time to talk? We have an hour or so before dinner."

Sven bowed. "Of course, my lady." He slapped Woden's shoulder. "Why don't you go and ready Ms. Cooper's bath and I'll bring her along to her suite as soon as we're done?"

He led Thea down to one of the more secluded terraced water gardens which overlooked the desert-facing side of the immense building. The palace contained many such places, designed as it was to provide everything the king and queen might need without them having to leave the security of their own walls.

"This is really pretty." Thea came to a stop in the center of the pink paved floor and stared up at the intricate marble fountain. "Is the water drinkable?"

"I believe it is, my lady. The palace has its own water supply from springs beneath the surface."

"It's like a fortress, isn't it? A beautiful fortress but still...Valhalla's recent history has not been peaceful." She looked back at him. "Because of the shortage of women and the falling birthrate, right?"

"And tribal conflicts. The present king's father did a great deal to unite the country and King Marcus is even more determined to make this land peaceful."

Sven moved from the archway to stand beside her. The delicate spray from the fountain gilded her skin, making him want to lean forward and lick it off.

"Sven, what did you mean about me being a hypocrite this morning?"

He sighed. Sometimes he wished she wasn't quite so smart or ready to take him on.

"I regret my words, my lady. Can we pretend I didn't say them?"

"No, we can't."

He sat on the edge of the fountain and looked up at her. By Thor's bones, she was indeed beautiful and he had nothing to lose. Either she would accept his culture and understand him, or she wouldn't. He drew in an unsteady breath.

"I was jealous."

"Jealous of Woden?"

"Aye."

"Because he touched me?"

Sven frowned. "He did more than touch you. He brought you to your woman's pleasure, more than once."

Her cheeks flushed. "Did he tell you that?"

"Nay. I know what you look like when you have been well serviced." He reached up to stroke the soft skin of her wrist. "That is how you looked this morning."

She bit down on her lip, her eyes troubled. "You're right. I am a hypocrite. I should not have let him touch me."

Sven frowned. "Why not? You are an unattached female. It is your right."

"Not where I come from."

"But you are on Valhalla, now. That is what males do for females."

She held his gaze. "It still felt wrong. At first, when I woke up and realized what was happening, I thought it was you."

He swallowed hard. "I wish it had been."

She attempted a smile. He realized she often tried to turn things into a joke or turn the question against him when he came too close. "Why? You were probably getting busy with the queen."

Sven stood up. "You are confusing two different things."

"So everyone keeps telling me." She walked back toward the door. Was she too embarrassed to continue the conversation? He had to make her stay. Sven cleared his throat.

"I apologize for calling you a hypocrite."

She stopped and slowly turned around. "You shouldn't. I'm the one who dumped you for doing the queen and then let a perfect stranger sex me up in the shower."

"You are too critical of yourself. As an unattached female you should revel in your sexuality."

"Yeah right, and you weren't jealous either."

Sven bowed. "Touché, my lady."

Her mouth quirked up at the corner as if she was trying not to laugh." I don't think that's a Valhallan expression."

"Nay, I picked it up from your Earth cartoons."

She smiled properly for the first time. "We're stuck here together, Sven, for the next few weeks. Can we at least try to be friends?"

He frowned. "I've never had a female friend."

"Well, here's your opportunity." She blew him a kiss. "I'll see you tomorrow."

"Aye, my lady, tomorrow."

Sven watched her leave and then sat back down on the edge of the fountain. He put his head in his hands and growled a few choice curses. His *friend*? He would never understand the workings of a woman's mind. He'd come to her, tried to open his heart and tell her how he felt. By Thor, he'd even admitted he was *jealous* and she'd still decided he wanted to be her friend.

"Is everything okay, Sven?"

He looked up to see the queen silhouetted in the doorway.

"With all due respect, My Queen, I am trying and failing to make Ms. Cooper understand that my relationship with you is not the same as the one I wish to have with her. I'm not sure if she simply doesn't understand or doesn't care."

Douglass nodded. "It's okay, Sven, I understand. Did Marcus tell you he is meeting with Thorlan the council leader tomorrow to ask about releasing you from your vows?"

Sven raised his head. "He is? I didn't know." A spark of hope ignited in his gut. "Perhaps Thea would welcome me if I were free."

"Perhaps she would."

"Or maybe the king is right and the mere idea that I touched you at all is unforgivable to a woman raised on Earth." Sven sighed and fixed his attention on the queen who was looking thoughtful. He frowned. He'd learned to fear that expression over the past year or so.

"My Queen?"

"Perhaps Ms. Cooper needs to see what's in front of her nose." The queen nodded. "I have to go find the king."

Sven stood up as she hurried away from him, a deep sense of unease clouding his senses. What in Thor's name was the queen going to do and how did it affect him and Thea?

After dinner, Thea wandered back up to her suite, her mind busy pondering Sven and his apology. Were he and Matt right that she didn't believe herself worthy to be loved? She thought back to her past relationships. The men she'd chosen to go out with tended to be the kind she knew would eventually hurt her. She tended to ignore the nice decent guys. Did she really feel so undeserving?

Thea stopped dead in the hallway. Just because her father had abandoned her and her mother sucked at relationships, didn't mean she had to as well. Perhaps having Sven as a friend would be a good way of learning how to love a man for himself rather than for what he could give or take from her. Not that Sven had seemed very keen on the idea. He'd looked positively stunned.

She opened the door to her suite and saw Woden sitting on the couch by the window strumming a musical instrument. He got up when he saw her.

"My lady, are you all right? You seem a little upset."

Thea sat down on the couch beside him. "I've just been thinking about all the men in my life and how much they suck."

Woden nodded wisely. "Aye, some males suck better than others."

Thea stared at him. "What?"

"I am agreeing with you. Some men are better at sucking a woman's breasts and pussy than others." He patted his chest. "I have been told I'm very thorough."

"Woden, is sex all you ever think about?"

He frowned and folded his arms across his bare chest. "Nay, my lady. I think about hunting and fighting as well."

"You're such a guy."

"And is that a good thing?"

Thea smiled. "You're pure male."

He grinned at her. "Now *that* I understand. Thank you for the compliment." He got to his feet and bowed. "Would you like to take your bath now?"

She let Woden bathe her and massage perfumed oil into her skin until she felt as relaxed as warm taffy. She even let him make her come twice without allowing guilt to overwhelm her pleasure or her yearning for it to be Sven. Now she lay naked on her stomach while he massaged her buttocks, his strong fingers deliberately penetrating her anus with every firm stroke. She turned her head to look at him.

"What is it with you Valhallan men and my ass?"

"When your male lovers on Earth service you, don't they make sure you can take them here easily too?" Woden added a third finger, making her squirm on the pale silk sheets.

"As I said before, on Earth it's usually only *one* lover, if you can find one."

Woden chuckled. "But how can one male satisfy a female? Why do you think the gods gave you enough openings to allow three cocks? One poor man would be exhausted by the end of the night."

An image of the queen and her bodyguards flashed in Thea's brain and she shivered. Woden continued to speak as he thumbed her swollen clit.

"Valhallan males know that it takes a woman longer to reach arousal. They understand that they can all play their part in making a female ready for her mate, even if they aren't mated themselves."

A clock chimed somewhere in the distance and the outer door to her suite opened with a rush of warm air. Woden kissed her shoulder.

"Let me see who it is. I'll be back in a moment."

Thea's eyes began to close. Woden touched her cheek.

"My lady, the king wishes to see you."

Thea opened one eye. "Now?"

"Aye, it is important. It concerns the queen."

She scrambled to sit up and Woden threw a thick cloak over her nakedness. One of the palace guards guided them along the deserted moonlit corridors at a fast pace. Having an excellent sense of direction, Thea soon recognized they weren't heading directly to the queen's chambers, but to the king's, which she hadn't yet seen. The wide doors opened to display the king, who inclined his head.

"Ah, Ms. Cooper. Thank you for joining me."

Thea stared at the king, who wore nothing but a tight fitting pair of leather pants. She grabbed at the edges of her cloak, suddenly aware of her nakedness and the fact that she was alone with two virile Valhallan males.

"Good evening, Sire. How can I help you?"

The king gestured to Woden, who guided her across the vast bedroom to stand beside him. She tried hard not to look at the massive bed covered in gray silk sheets and fur coverings.

"The queen came to me this evening and asked if I would allow you to watch with me."

Thea swallowed hard. "Watch what, Sire?"

"This." The king pulled the silk drapes away to reveal a mirror which looked down on the queen's bedroom. Thea tried to back up but found her way blocked by Woden's muscular frame.

"I don't think I should be looking at this at all, Sire. I feel like a peeping Tom."

"It is all right, Ms. Cooper. They cannot see you."

In the room below, the queen lay back on her cream silk pillows, her head pillowed in Sven's lap. Bron knelt between her legs, his mouth working her sex and Harlan licked and plucked at her nipples. Beside Thea, the king groaned.

"My queen looks so beautiful being pleasured, does she not?"

Thea bit her lip. What the hell was she supposed to say? Woden cleared his throat.

"She is magnificent, Sire. I would be honored to pleasure her myself."

Thea tensed. Was Woden crazy? Surely the king would find his remarks offensive?

"Thank you, Woden. She is indeed memorable in the throes of climaxing, her nipples tight, her pussy covered in cream and open for my cock."

Thea tried to put some distance between the king and herself but Woden had her pressed up against the mirror. Was the king some kind of pervert who could only get off by watching other men fornicate with his wife? Was this what Sven had been trying to tell her?

Thea couldn't stop staring at Sven's beautiful body as he caressed the queen's hair and occasionally kissed her mouth when she thrashed around, caught up in yet another climax. His expression was distant as if he wasn't fully participating in the orgy of pleasure surrounding him. Was he thinking of Thea as he was forced to pleasure his king's wife? A thread of pure lust pushed through her anxiety.

Woden groaned, slid his hands beneath her cloak and captured her breasts. His thumbs brushed her erect nipples and she trembled. Below them, Bron moved to one side, momentarily exposing the queen's sex to the watchers above. He kissed the queen's knee, his cock rubbing against her outer thigh and thrust his fingers in and out of her until she writhed on the bed.

Harlan slid a hand down over the queen's flat stomach and fingered her clit in time to Bron's long measured finger thrusts. Thea could see his cock now, stiff and glistening with pre-cum as he pleasured the queen.

The king leaned closer against the mirrored glass, his breathing harsh, one hand buried down the front of his leather pants working his shaft.

"By Odin, she will be well serviced tonight."

Woden's hand slipped between Thea's legs. She was so wet, her folds parted easily to let his fingers enter her. Sven got off the bed and retrieved a gold chest from the window seat. Despite his apparent lack of interest, he was aroused, his shaft thick and stiff beneath the thin silk covering his groin. Thea tensed as he returned to the bed and sat between the queen's widespread thighs. Woden nipped at her ear.

"You see? Valhallan men understand how to make a woman ready to take a male. Sven will fill her now." Thea tried to close her eyes. "She will need to be filled well. The king is a big man."

"So is Sven." She tried to push away from Woden. "I really don't want to see this."

The king glanced at her, his expression uncompromising. "Ms. Cooper, you really do."

She forced herself to stare at Sven's naked back. Perhaps the king was right. Seeing Sven fuck the queen might make it easier for her to hate him forever and get over him quicker. She tensed as Sven opened the jeweled box and withdrew several objects.

Woden whispered in her ear. "Sven is preparing the queen for her mating. He will fill her with the two pleasure givers so that she will take the king with ease."

"Take the king?"

"Aye."

"But the king is standing right next to us!"

141

"Not for long." Woden's fingers moved against her mound, sliding between her swollen lips. "As soon as his mate is well aroused by her servers, he will go down to her."

Thea took a deep breath and removed Woden's hand from between her legs, difficult when her body was on the verge of a climax. "The servers don't make love to her, do they?"

The king laughed as he stepped out of his leather pants to display the biggest erection Thea had ever seen. He wrapped his fingers around his shaft and added a thick gold cock ring.

"Douglass is my wife. I am the only male who gives her my seed."

She stared at him as he continued to play with his cock, his gaze fixed on the scene below him. "So Sven hasn't…"

"Mated with my queen? Nay."

Thea shivered as the king dropped a hand on her shoulder.

"Ms. Cooper, please try to understand. Sven is only doing what any Valhallan male should, offering his services to a fertile female. Does that offend you?"

"I'm not sure, Sire. It's just not what I'm used to."

Hadn't Sven told her that he'd only mated with one woman? What the hell was going on? If he hadn't meant the queen, who had he been mated with? Thea tried hard not to look at the king's magnificent nakedness, although he was so large it was difficult to see anything else. He sighed.

"Take Ms. Cooper back to her suite, Woden, and make sure you give her pleasure. She has a lot to think about."

He bowed and headed for a discreet door next to the mirrored glass. Moments later, he joined the queen on the large bed. Douglass held out her arms to welcome him, her expression radiant. Sven and his companions left the room and Thea closed her eyes. Her body throbbed with sensual heat. How would it feel to be Sven or Harlan or Bron, denied the opportunity to finish what they had started? How did they bear it? Did that explain the intensity in Sven's eyes when he made love to her, that desire for completion, to possess a woman of his own?

"My lady?"

She allowed Woden to accompany her back to her suite. It was completely dark in the palace now, the night air slicing through wide halls turned cold and unwelcoming. Thea drew in a breath.

"How do you stand it?"

"What, my lady?"

"Not being allowed to make love after all that stimulation."

Woden helped her out of her cloak and tucked her into bed. He brought her a silver cup filled with fragrant apple-scented wine and sat beside her.

"For us, I suppose it is better than the alternative of having no female to touch at all. Also by learning to please a woman we gains skills that hopefully in time will help us be chosen as true mates."

Thea clutched at the wine cup. "But don't you think it's cruel?"

He raised his eyebrows. "Why is it cruel? If I want to come, I can take care of it myself. If I'm lucky, the woman I pleasure will take care of me too."

"God, it is so hard for me to understand."

Woden took the cup from her and kissed the top of her head. "It is just different. The men on your planet are different." He chuckled as he kissed her again. "By Thor, sometimes I wish I lived on your planet and could have all the women I wanted."

Thea touched his cheek. "But then you'd end up just like them, so used to having sex that it wouldn't mean anything to you anymore."

Woden looked thoughtful. "I hadn't thought of that. Perhaps our way is better after all." He pulled back the covers and slid into bed beside Thea. "And now I have to pleasure you as the king commanded."

Thea shivered as he stroked her breasts, her thoughts in an uproar. If Sven were from Earth, maybe she would be justified in accusing him of two-timing her. But he was a Valhallan. A man acting as his culture demanded. To her private, selfish satisfaction, he hadn't seemed to be enjoying himself much with the queen either. Harlan and Bron had done most of the pleasuring. Did his feelings for her affect his feelings for the queen?

Woden groaned as he suckled at her breast, his hand cupping her pussy. "Relax, my lady. Let me bring you joy."

Was she wrong to judge Sven by her standards? In many ways the Valhallan men were far better than their counterparts on Earth. They adored women and truly believed their purpose in life was to give a female pleasure. Okay, so they did this because they wanted heirs, but still, Sven had tried to be honest with her—up to a point.

Thea gave up the struggle to think as Woden's long fingers slid inside her and allowed herself to slip away into warm, sleepy sexual fulfillment.

Chapter Nine

ℰ⌀

Sven glanced around the queen's bedroom, his expression grim. Despite the fact that everything looked normal, something was in the air and he wasn't in the mood to accept excuses. His irate gaze settled on the queen.

"My lady, what exactly is going on?"

Douglass grinned at him. She sat on the end of her bed, feeding baby Thor. Her long dark hair was braided and hung over one shoulder. Thor held onto it with one small hand as he suckled.

"I've arranged a surprise for Ms. Cooper and I thought you might like to be the one who tells her about it."

"What kind of surprise?"

"Well, it's kind of two-pronged," the queen winked, "if you get my meaning."

Sven folded his arms across his chest. "Nay, I don't."

Douglass sighed. "Sven, don't be an asshole. You'll like it, I promise you."

He took a deliberate step forward. "My Queen, I can still take you over my knee and spank you."

She stuck her tongue out at him. "Ooh, I'm really scared. You know how much I like a good spanking."

Sven ground his teeth so loudly that Harlan winced. "My lady, are you going to tell me what is going on or not?"

"Oh, my plan. The king has arranged for the Super Bowl to be aired here on Valhalla, isn't that amazing?"

"The Earth football game?"

"Yeah and I know Ms. Cooper is a big fan, so here's what we're going to do. The king and I will invite her and Woden to watch it with all of us. During the game, we, that is me and Marcus will disappear, and leave you lot to pleasure Ms. Cooper."

"Are you mad? Ms. Cooper will never agree to that."

"I think she will. According to the king she got very turned on watching us last night."

Sven's hands fisted by his sides.

"She watched me *pleasure* you? And you think she'll ever want to see me again?"

"Apparently, she didn't want to watch you at all. The king made her."

Sven struggled to breathe. "My Queen, what have you done?"

Douglass looked right back at him. "Shown the woman you love exactly what being my server implied."

"She already knew that. It didn't make any difference to her dumping me."

"No, she didn't."

Sven frowned at the queen. "I told her."

"You obviously weren't very specific. She didn't know that only the king gets to fully mate with me."

"But I told her I had only ever mated with one female."

Bron cleared his throat. "Forgive me for asking this—but you told Ms. Cooper about your wife?"

"Nay, I..." Sven stopped speaking and simply stared at the queen and the two other men. "I said that a Valhallan only fully mates with one woman."

"But you didn't mention you'd ever taken a woman to wife."

"Those memories are painful for me. I do not share them lightly."

"So it's highly likely that Ms. Cooper got confused and thought the only woman you were having was me."

Sven sat down heavily on the side of the bed. "She couldn't have been so misguided, could she?"

"Maybe you'd better ask her yourself."

Sven groaned and dropped his head into his hands. "How can I do that? After what she saw last night, she is probably packing her bags."

"No, she isn't."

"How do you know that?"

The queen cleared her throat. "Um, because she's standing right in front of you?"

Sven slowly raised his head and saw Thea. He got unsteadily to his feet and bowed.

My lady?"

Thea turned to the queen. "Can I borrow him for a minute?"

"You can borrow him for as long as you like, just make sure you return him in the condition you found him."

"Like a library book?"

The queen laughed. "Oh my god, finally, someone who gets my jokes."

Sven glowered at them both. "I still don't find you amusing, My Queen."

She waved a hand at him. "Go away, Sven. Talk to Thea."

Sven led Thea out of the queen's suite and down to the fountain garden where they had met the night before. This time, he remained by the exit, his arms folded over his chest. Thea walked away from him and circled the fountain, her fingers trailing in the water.

"Can I ask you something, Sven?"

He nodded, his gaze fixed on the intricately colored tiles in front of him.

"When you said you had only mated with one woman, what exactly did you mean?"

"What I said."

Thea took a deep calming breath.

"And when you say 'mate' you mean have full sexual intercourse with."

"I mean mate."

"So have you mated with the queen?"

He still wouldn't look at her, his attention fixed on his big bare feet.

"It depends what you mean."

"Sven, you just said mating only meant one thing!"

He shrugged but didn't look up. Thea circled the fountain again, her thoughts in turmoil.

"Let me put it another way. Have you ever come inside the queen's body?"

"Aye."

A wave of misery shot through her. Perhaps she wasn't as ready to be as understanding as she'd hoped.

"So the king was wrong and he has been cuckolded."

"I would never do that." This time he did look at her, his dark gaze direct and uncompromising. She held up her hands in a pleading gesture.

"Sven, help me out here. The king said he is the only male who gives the queen his seed, so how come you're saying something different?"

He scowled at her as if she was deliberately playing dumb. "The king is her *mate*, I am only her server."

"But you've had sex with her."

"I've helped arouse her so that the king can fertilize her more easily, if that is what you mean."

148

Thea stared at him as all the conversations she'd had with the Valhallan men coalesced in her mind. "Excuse me if this sounds way too personal, but a female has enough, um, 'places' to take three cocks."

"Aye."

"But only depositing your seed in one of them will result in her becoming pregnant."

"Aye."

Thea walked up to Sven who was watching her intently. "So you're saying that you've had the queen in all ways but one."

"Aye."

She punched him so hard on the chest that she hurt her hand. "So why didn't you just say so?"

He frowned. "I am the queen's server, not her mate. It's obvious."

Despite the throb of her knuckles, she punched him again. "Not to me!"

For a moment, she allowed her forehead to rest against his broad chest.

"Then who did you mate with?"

Silence greeted her question. She straightened until she could see his face.

"Sven?"

He let out his breath. "My wife."

"You're married?"

"It was a long time ago. She died a year after our wedding."

"That's awful." She touched his cheek and he stepped away from her, presenting his broad back. Her hand dropped to her side.

"She was a small woman and my son was too big for her to birth."

Thea kept quiet. How long had it been since Sven had spoken of his wife?

"I should not have married her."

She stroked his back, felt him quiver and then tense as if he couldn't bear the intimate contact with her. She withdrew her hand, torn between offering him comfort and giving him space to regain control.

"Thank you for answering my questions. At least I feel I know where I stand now. I have a lot to think about."

"Aye."

"Perhaps I'll see you later?"

"Aye."

Thea pasted on a smile, even though he wasn't looking at her.

"Okay, then, I'll go. I'll tell the queen you'll be along later, all right?"

Without waiting for his reply, which was unlikely to be more than 'aye' anyway, she turned and went back the way she'd come. She wasn't kidding. She really did need time to think things through. Was she prepared to accept that Sven meant what he said about his relationship with her being special, or was the whole idea of Valhallan male sexuality and the way they interacted with females just too much for her to take?

She paused in the hallway and looked down into one of the courtyards below her where the king and Harlan were practicing their ax play. The king didn't seem to pleasure any other woman but the queen. Once a Valhallan man was married did he only get to sleep with his wife? She'd have to find a polite way of finding the answer to that very intriguing question after her lunch.

Thea knocked nervously on the door of the queen's suite. It was already evening and she hadn't seen Sven all day.

Instead of worrying herself half to death about what she was going to do, she'd taken the opportunity to go out with the king and investigate the palace security more closely. The complex nature of the Valhallan systems and the upgrades she had suggested had certainly occupied her mind for most of the afternoon. She hadn't found a way to ask the king about his sexual behavior since his marriage, somehow it hadn't seemed appropriate.

The invitation to join the king and the queen in the royal suite for a special event that night had made her slightly nervous. Last time she'd been invited into the royal suite, she'd seen a rather too intimate view of the couple and way too much of the king so she wasn't keen to repeat the experience. Sometimes the Valhallans open attitude to sex still surprised her. She straightened as Bron opened the door, a beaming smile on his face.

"Ms. Cooper, I'm so glad you have come." He stepped aside and bowed, the lamplight glinting off his blond hair and the armbands he wore around his finely sculptured biceps. He wasn't as big as the other bodyguards, but he had a lean, elegant strength that reminded Thea of a jaguar or a leopard.

"Thanks, Bron. I'm not quite sure *why* I'm here, though."

A roar of noise drowned out the rest of her words. Bron sighed. "They are already taking sides and drinking too much mead. Perhaps your presence will encourage them to sit down and behave themselves."

Thea kept walking, her gaze drawn to the huge screen at one end of the massive room. The rest of the Valhallan bodyguards and the queen sat on silken cushions on the floor watching intently. Harlan held baby Thor up against one shoulder and Sven was talking animatedly with the king. Thea pressed a hand to her chest.

"Oh my god, it's the Super Bowl."

The queen stood up, her eyes shining. "Yeah, isn't it great? I asked Marcus if he could set it up for us and he liaised with Matt Logan and he did it! It's not often my team gets to play in the Super Bowl."

Thea frowned. "You're a Raiders fan aren't you?"

Douglass smoothed down her black and silver tunic. "You noticed."

"I support the 49ers."

"Really?" The queen's eyes narrowed and she stuck out her hand. "Well, may the best team win."

Thea shook it hard. "They will."

"I know they will."

For a moment they locked gazes and then both laughed. Douglass took Thea's arm and led her toward the king.

"Come and sit down. I'll make sure Marcus keeps us apart if we get too rowdy."

Thea settled herself awkwardly into one of the huge silk pillows between the king and Sven. She couldn't believe she was actually getting to watch the Super Bowl way out here. She'd been devastated when she'd realized she would miss the first clash between the Bay area's local teams for over a hundred years.

The king nudged her. "We have popcorn and mead, no beer unfortunately, but there will be pizza later if the palace cooks work out how to make it."

"That's great, Sire. I really appreciate the effort you've all gone to."

He chuckled. "Please call me Marcus. I did it mainly for the queen, but it was an honor to please you too. You have given so much to my planet."

Thea shrugged. "I'm only doing my job."

"But you didn't particularly want to come to Valhalla did you?"

Thea cast a quick glance to her left where Sven was listening intently. "That was because of a stupid misunderstanding. I'm glad I came, I really am."

The king grunted as Douglass jabbed him in the ribs.

"Be quiet, Marcus. The game is about to start."

Thea whooped as her team ran out onto the field and then booed when they were followed by the Raiders. Harlan pointed at the players.

"Why do these men need so much padding? When we play this kind of game on Valhalla, we don't wear full body armor."

"It's a very violent game, Harlan," Thea said. "These guys get paid a lot of money to play so no one wants to see them get injured."

"They get paid?"

"More money than you can imagine."

Harlan settled the prince in his arms. "Perhaps I should start training some of our youths to play this game seriously."

"That's a great idea." Douglass poked the king again. "Marcus, tell the Council to set up a training program."

The king groaned. "Yes dear, I'll add it to the other three hundred requests you have made since our return."

Thea glanced around. All the talk about padding had made her conscious that she was the only person in the room wearing her official yellow jumpsuit. All the Valhallan males were clothed in either leather pants or tight white loincloths like the one Woden usually wore. Their chests were bare, their muscled torsos gleamed with oil and the faint scent of spicy fragrances.

Surreptitiously she tugged down the zipper of her suit a couple of inches. Was it getting warmer or was she just feeling overdressed? The referee marched to the center of the field and Thea forgot about the males surrounding her and concentrated on the game.

To her delight, after the first two quarters, her team was ahead. Douglass complained loudly to the king about some of the referees' decisions while Thea just smirked. During a lull in the spirited conversation, Sven handed her another cup of mead and she drank it down in one long swallow.

"Would you like more?"

She turned to study Sven properly for the first time. He looked as if he hadn't slept properly for days. Her heart twisted in her chest.

"Yeah, more would be great."

He got up to retrieve the jug of mead that was circulating among the other men, giving a splendid view of his ass encased in thin white silk and the huge bulge of his cock when he turned back toward her. He kept his gaze on the cup while he filled it and handed it back to her.

She drank again, the sweet honeyed taste perfect to quench her thirst. She had no idea how much alcohol was actually in it, but reckoned it couldn't be that much, seeing as so far she felt just fine. Sven sat down beside her again; his large body sprawled out against the silken cushions.

"Ms. Cooper, are you hot?"

She tore her attention away from the terrible commercials and stared at Sven.

"Yeah, a bit."

Sven eyed her jumpsuit. "We are quite alone here. No one else will come in. You could take it off."

"The king and queen are here, as are Bron, Harlan and Woden. That scarcely means we're alone."

He shrugged. "Woden and I have already seen your body and Harlan and Bron would probably enjoy the sight. So what is the problem?"

The king stood up, his arm around the queen who held his baby son. He bowed to Thea.

"Excuse us, Ms. Cooper. We are going to watch the rest of the game in my suite. Please feel free to stay here and enjoy our Valhallan hospitality."

Thea scrambled to her feet and stared hard at the queen. "Are you sure?" She glanced around at the rest of the smiling Valhallan men. "Shouldn't they be with you?"

"They all have the evening off. What they choose to do with their free time is entirely up to them and *entirely* okay with me." The queen winked at Thea. "In fact, I'll be very disappointed if I hear you haven't been *completely* satisfied. Have fun, Thea."

Thea watched the royal couple leave. Had Douglass just given them permission to have their own orgy? From the expectant expressions on the men's faces, she had. Thea sat back down, her heart thumping, her body warming with anticipation. Images of the queen being attended to by her servers flashed through her mind. Did she want that? Would it be a way of finding out whether she could come to terms with Valhallan sexual customs?

"My lady?"

Thea jumped as Sven touched her knee.

"Would you like another drink? The third quarter is about to start."

"Yeah, I mean, yes please, that would be great." Thea handed over her empty cup as Harlan settled into the cushion on her right that the king had vacated. Bron and Woden took up positions behind Sven and Harlan. After a little while, everyone returned their attention to the game and Thea started to relax. The mead had made her feel a bit fuzzy and more laid back than usual. It was an unusually pleasant experience.

"Are you going to take that off?"

Harlan's whisper made her jump as he tugged on the zipper of her suit. She drew in a calming breath, hoped her voice didn't squeak.

"Okay."

She shut her eyes as Harlan unzipped her suit and helped her out of it. A low murmur of male appreciation greeted the appearance of her matching pink bra and panties set.

"I told you she was beautiful."

Woden sounded very pleased with himself. Thea resisted the desire to cover herself with her hands and slowly opened her eyes. No one was looking at her anymore, all attention had returned to the screen. After a long moment, she tried to forget that she was half-naked and focus on the game.

She shivered as Harlan slid his arm around her and cupped her breast, his thumb found her silk-covered nipple and circled it. Thea kept her gaze on the big screen, resisting the urge to squeeze her legs together as tightly as she could. Harlan's other hand slid onto her thigh, his fingers outlining the high cut of her panties and then came to rest over her mound. Heat built between Thea's thighs and the slow exciting pulse of arousal shuddered through her. This was like all her fantasies rolled into one. Great football, plenty of pizza and several hunky men whose idea of fun was giving her the best orgasms of her life.

As the commercial break started, Sven leaned toward her, his gaze fixed on Harlan's stroking fingers.

"Does he please you, my lady?"

"A bit."

Harlan laughed, his fingers tightening over her pussy. "She lies, she is already wet, Sven. Do you want me to show you?"

Sven held Thea's gaze. "Aye, show me."

Harlan glanced up at Bron and Woden. "Woden, sit behind your lady, Bron come and help me."

Sven sat back on the cushions, one hand, idly stroking his cock. Thea tensed as Woden drew her back to sit between his open thighs, the thick, hot press of his shaft moved against her lower spine. Harlan knelt in front of her, his hands on her knees.

"Let me see how wet you are, my lady. Let your mate see how much you desire him."

Thea licked her lips. Was this really what she wanted? She remembered the queen being spread wide like this by her servers, the ecstasy on her face mirrored by the king's as he watched her being prepared for him. She glanced at Sven, his attention was completely focused on her, his expression avid, his cock filling out as he watched.

Hell, yes, she'd do it if it meant that Sven finally understood that she was trying to accept his sexual customs and would soon be inside her. She allowed her knees to part. Harlan groaned.

"See, Sven, her panties are soaked with her cream." He leaned forward and licked the silk, his agile tongue nudging her clit until it swelled and showed through the thin fabric. "I can smell her arousal."

"Lick her again, Harlan." Sven's voice was barely above a growl. "Suckle her breasts Bron and Woden."

Thea gasped at the triple assault on her most sensitive parts. Her hips jerked forward in rhythm to Harlan's delicate licks and the harder sucks of the other men to her tight nipples. Her fantasies and imagination hadn't prepared her for the intensity of three men pleasuring her. Desire tightened and coiled low in her stomach. When Sven roughly kissed her, she climaxed, moaning into his mouth as he deliberately bit down on her lip.

Hey, the game's restarting."

Thea opened her eyes as all the guys abruptly ceased touching her. She lay back against the pillows, the fabric of her bra and panties soaked through and cooling against her skin. She was panting, every nerve in her body craving the sensations they had aroused in her, screaming for completion. Sven moved away from her too, his gaze fixed on the game, his hand lingering on her shoulder.

By the time she managed to take note that the Raiders had equalized, another commercial break occurred and the men turned their attention back to her. As the game wore on, she didn't know whether to laugh or to be insulted. Soon, her panties and bra disappeared and her body was open to them. Their attention to her during the breaks was total and exquisite and then it took the whole of the next few plays on the football field for her to recover. Her body hummed with pleasure and she gloried in the sight of Sven watching her, the intent look in his eyes as the other men brought her closer and closer to completion.

She moaned as a naked Woden took his turn between her thighs, licking her now sensitive clit, three of his oiled fingers buried in her ass. She luxuriated in the extreme sensations. She no longer knew what her limits were, she only knew that Sven would insist she experienced every sensation and then would push her even further.

"See how ready she is for you, Sven." Bron slid one slim finger inside her channel making her back arch. "She is so wet, your cock will slide inside her easily. Should we prepare her for you now?"

Sven grunted his assent, one hand working his shaft. Thea tried to catch his gaze, not easy when he stared at her pussy as Bron and Woden turned her into mush. With a harsh sound, Sven knelt up and brushed his silk-covered cock against her lips. She opened her mouth, desperate for a taste of him. He thrust into her, groaning as her lips surrounded him. She sucked him as hard as she could, determined to make him share her building arousal. How did she look to him, her body flushed and aroused, straining against the pillows, open to his gaze, with no place to hide her true sexual nature?

She stiffened as Bron and Woden slid thick oiled leather dildos inside both of her passages. She felt impossibly full and climaxed again, moaning against the thick pressure of Sven's shaft as he fucked her mouth. Bron licked her clit and then sat back on his heels to observe her widespread legs.

"She looks well prepared for you now. Despite her narrow hips, she can take a man deep."

"I know." Sven sounded hoarse, his hips jerking as he worked his cock to the rhythm of her mouth.

Distantly, Thea heard the referee's whistle. Sven tried to pull away but she set her teeth lightly against his shaft. He froze over her, his thick hot cock motionless in her mouth. When she tried to release him, he refused to pull out further, forcing her to hold him deep and feel the constant trickle of his pre-cum down her throat as she frantically swallowed. God, she'd never felt so full before, all her orifices stuffed to the brink, her clit pumping like a second heartbeat.

"Turn her over, Harlan."

Thea gasped as she was rotated onto her hands and knees, her mouth still surrounding Sven's cock. He wrapped a hand around his shaft and eased it out of her mouth. He bent down until he could meet her gaze.

"Whose cock would you like to taste while I fuck your ass?"

"I get a choice?"

Sven grimaced. "If I had to choose, it would only be me. But I only have one cock and I know you would enjoy being penetrated by more than one man."

Thea struggled to breath. "How do you know that?"

"I saw your holo-screen, remember? You and the two weak Earth men." He kissed her savagely. "Well now I honor your fantasies and offer you three strong Valhallan males instead."

"How am I supposed to choose? They are all so cute."

Sven caught her chin in his fingers. "Choose quickly or they'll all want in. Do you think you can take three cocks in your mouth?"

Thea gazed into his lust-filled eyes and realized he was serious. Her pussy flooded with cream at the salacious thought. Sven's gaze narrowed.

"Quickly, my lady, or you'll be sorry."

"I'll choose Woden, then."

"I am honored, my lady."

Woden moved to take Sven's place, his cock already dripping wet and ready for her. Sven moved behind her, his hands grasping her hips. He pulled out the thick leather dildo. Warm oil trickled down between her cheeks. She tensed as she felt the first nudge of the crown of his cock against the tight bud of her ass.

"Woden, when I give you leave, slide your cock into her mouth."

"Aye, Sven." Woden wrapped one hand around the thick base of his shaft and brought it to her lips. His pre-cum spilled into her slightly open mouth, his taste, less salty and distinct from Sven's.

"Take our cocks, Thea."

He must have nodded to Woden because they both began to move, their cocks sliding inside her together until they were both buried deep within her. At the double penetration, Thea started to shake, setting off a series of climaxes that exploded inside her womb.

Sven gripped her hips even harder. "By Thor, she squeezes me like an ironclad fist."

"Aye, her mouth is tight around me too," Woden said hoarsely. Thea shuddered as they began to work her between them, Sven's strong thrusts pushing Woden's shaft deeper and deeper down her throat. Two tugs on her nipples made her realize Bron and Harlan had joined in her torment and that she was helpless to resist.

Her climaxes began to blend together until she thought she would explode. Nothing existed but the pleasure of being filled by the two men. She allowed herself to experience a deep-seated desire to be taken, to be possessed, a desire that she would never have acted upon until Sven had shown her the way. Sven's breathing grew guttural, his strokes shorter and harder as his fingers dug into her hips.

He shouted as he climaxed, swiftly followed by Woden. Thea swallowed hard as his cum pumped down her throat, aware of Sven's seed flooding into her at the same time. Woden pulled out and Sven slumped over her, his breathing as ragged as her own. He rolled her over onto her back.

"Did we please you, my lady?"

Thea simply stared at him, her body still reeling from the most salacious sexual experience of her life. His smile was all teeth and satisfied alpha male. He slid his fingers down to touch her clit and then lower to circle the thick leather dildo.

"I would be honored to spill my seed in you, my lady."

Dammit, his cock was already filling out again. Thea licked her lips. Could she take anymore, and more importantly, could she risk missing the end of the football game? Sven bent to kiss her clit.

"We have all evening, my lady. Perhaps we should watch the last five minutes of the game?"

Thea struggled to sit up. There were only five minutes left? How the hell had that happened? The two teams were still level. Harlan's fingers curved around her breast and she smacked them away.

Sven couldn't take his eyes off Thea as she refocused her attention on the game. Her skin was flushed and glowing from the sex and his seed still flowed from her ass. She seemed to have forgotten about the thick dildo stuffed in her pussy. He drew her back between his outstretched legs, anchoring her buttocks against his erection. She didn't stop him taking charge of her body, nor did she take her gaze from the screen. Sven bit back a smile. Her focus was admirable for a woman.

The game inched with painful slowness toward the end. Both sides gridlocked in a draw, neither able to dominate the other. To his astonishment, Sven began to appreciate the skill level, the sheer determination on the players exhausted faces and their immense drive to be victorious.

"The queen is right. We must bring this sport to Valhalla. Our young men would excel at this."

Harlan nodded his agreement. "I'll talk to the Council as soon as I can."

"Ssh!"

Sven grunted as Thea elbowed him in the stomach.

"They can scarcely hear me, my lady. We are thousands of miles away!"

She turned to glare at him and tapped her forehead. "Yes they can, they can sense your negativity, so be quiet. This is my team's last chance to score."

By now, Sven had developed an excellent understanding of how the game was played. Smiling, he placed one hand over the exposed end of the dildo and began to move it gently back and forth. Thea's skin flushed even more and she leaned forward as her team lined up for the final play. As the team crept closer to the opposition's line, Sven increased the speed and pressure of his strokes.

Thea moaned and placed her hand over his slow moving fingers.

"God, Sven, this isn't helping, I can't concentrate, I can't…"

A grinning San Francisco player caught the ball and crossed the line into the end zone, Thea screamed and tried to get to her feet.

"Oh no, my lady. You are not getting away from me now."

Sven shoved the dildo deep and kept her locked against him as she climaxed again and again. Before she could protest, he rolled on top of her, pulled out the soaked dildo and drove his cock inside her. She gripped his shoulders and planted her feet on his hips willing him on, forcing him to stay deep and hard inside her. By Thor, he could feel every pulsing inch of her channel clamping around his aching flesh. He forgot finesse and pounded into her, his balls slapping against her with every hard, grinding stroke. Her cries only made him work harder, to force yet another response from her to make her realize he was the only man who would ever be able to satisfy her like this.

He felt another climax build, the answering response in his balls and let his cum pour into her in thick pulsing waves. It felt so good to be inside his woman, filling her with his cock and his seed, knowing he'd made her scream in ecstasy and cling to him as though she would never let him go. He could only hope to stay like this forever, his body linked to hers and his scent smeared over her skin. Surely she would feel the same. She couldn't possibly leave him now, could she?

When Thea finally managed to roll Sven off her, the other men had gone. She stared at his recumbent form and then kicked him. He groaned and covered his eyes with the back of his hand.

"Sven Magnusson, did you set this whole thing up just to get into my pants again or was it the queen's idea?"

"My lady, I am too weak to answer such difficult questions. Give me a moment."

She nudged him again. "I've had about ten orgasms this afternoon and you've only managed a couple. I'm the one who should be exhausted, not you."

He opened one eye and glared at her. "A man's orgasm is different. It is more powerful and draining than you can imagine."

She grinned at him. "Poor little Sven, worn out after five minutes of fucking."

With a roar, he rolled over and covered her again. "We will see who is the strongest, my lady. You will be the one who is begging for mercy in the hours before dawn."

Thea opened her legs to accommodate his hips and moaned as his cock slid deep inside her. He'd taught her more about her sexual needs that she had ever imagined. He'd also made her understand that being erotically satisfied by more than one man was perfectly acceptable on Valhalla. He shifted position and drew her ankles up over his shoulders.

"I fear you aren't paying attention, my lady. Are you too tired to fuck?"

She gazed up at him, relished his strength and the sensual understanding in his lust-filled brown eyes. He slowly leaned into her, letting the weight of his lower torso press his cock deep inside her. She wanted to close her eyes against the exquisite sensation, but forced herself to stare back at him, let him see her pleasure in her eyes.

He shivered and licked his lips. "If you keep looking at me like that, tonight I will truly run out of come."

She gasped as he slid out and bent his head to her pussy. His mouth was incredibly gentle as he licked at her thick cream. He looked up at her, his lips wet with her juices. "Perhaps this will have to sustain me instead."

She reached down to stroke his hair and he turned his head to nuzzle her hand. Something inside her melted, gave in, flowered. She tugged on his thick red hair.

"Please Sven, make love to me, I want you so badly."

He went still, his breath warm on her thigh and then rose above her.

"That, my lady, would be an honor."

Chapter Ten

ဢ

Thea groaned and rolled over onto her stomach. It was official, Sven was the best lover in the known universe and she would never be able to move again. She reached out a hand, brushed silken sheets but thankfully no aroused man parts. She was in her own bed where Sven had eventually carried her after several more mind-blowing orgasms which had made walking impossible.

She needed a bath. She also needed time to think. Sven and the other Valhallan men had showed her exactly what being a female on Valhalla could mean. Now all she had to do was decide whether she could accept that or not. With a groan, she dragged herself to the edge of the bed and almost fell onto the thick rug on the marbled floor.

Her bathroom smelled of flowers and perfumed rose oil. She smiled as she discovered someone had already run her a bath, the surface scattered with flower petals and surrounded by soft candles. Perfect for thinking. Perfect for her tired muscles.

She lay back with a sigh and focused on the candlelight. She had to make a decision. The easiest thing to do would be to leave Valhalla, go back to Earth and find a new boyfriend. She frowned at the rapidly disappearing bubbles. After being appreciated by the Valhallans, she doubted that one Earth man would do the trick any more. Hadn't all her fantasies involved more than one man? Hadn't she been secretly ashamed of her high sexual libido? Not any more. The Valhallans thought her magnificent and perfectly womanly.

But what if she chose to stay? Marcus and Douglass were determined to make Valhalla a place where women were considered equal to men. Since the fertility issues had been worked out, the population would soon begin to multiply. And in the meantime, Thea was sure she could persuade a few of her pals to contemplate life on a planet where it was a man's primary duty to keep his woman sexually satisfied.

Would Sven be happy if she stayed? She smiled dreamily, her head angled back against the edge of the bath. She imagined he would and she also reckoned she would be able to persuade him to let her work with the king on improving Valhallan security until the rest of the planet got with the program. Reluctantly, she got out of the bath and blew out the candles. There, decision made. She'd talk to Sven, ask his opinion and stay, whatever he said.

Woden had obviously been in and laid out her clothes near the bath. She dressed in a silky two piece pantsuit before pulling her hated yellow regulation jumpsuit on over it. The palace seemed quiet as she opened the door to her suite and peered down the wide hallway. It was late morning, the bodyguards were probably training, which was where Thea should be. The king and queen and the rest of the population were probably napping or making love.

Thea set off down the hall, scanned the odd person she passed, answered salutations and even remembered to smile as she greeted them. Matt would be so proud. She stopped walking. He was the only person she would truly miss from Earth. She decided to call him on the link that very night to apologize and tell him her plans.

She glanced up as a movement on the stairway that led to the king and queen's apartments caught her attention. A woman carrying a heavily wrapped bundle headed down the stairs, her face hidden in a shawl. Thea moved up the steps toward her.

"Can I help you with something?"

A hand shot out and caught her squarely in the chest. She fell backward, struck the stone steps and ended up in a tangled heap back at the bottom of the stairs. She sprang to her feet, cursing as her ankle buckled.

"Hey!"

The cloaked figure ran toward a constricted opening in the wall and another flight of stairs. Ignoring the pain in her side, Thea started after her. The spiral stairway was hewn out of pale gray rock and seemed endless. She lost count of the number of stairs she pounded down, her breathing became labored, her gasps echoing in the rapidly narrowing passageway. The lamps disappeared, leaving her in a moist darkness that indicated she was either underground or near water.

She stopped running, heard the wail of a child and a sharp command. Dread seized her. Whose child was that? Could it be the young prince?

Thea crept forward more carefully now, trying to sense her surroundings. Just below her, a murmur of voices seemed to indicate she'd reached her prey. What should she do now? Go back and alert the other guards or move forward? With a swift prayer to all the gods of Valhalla and the universe, she decided to go on.

Surprise was on her side, but she wasn't prepared for the four men who surrounded the woman and the child. She fought hard, used her feet and hands and had the satisfaction of seeing at least one of the men go down before she was caught in a stranglehold, a knife to her throat. A thin trickle of blood stained her tunic.

A bearded man looked down at her.

"This is one of the Earth delegation." He squeezed her breast. "Nice tits."

An older guy, his face lined and worn, stepped forward, his expression worried.

"Raven, we should leave her here, we'll only bring more trouble down on ourselves."

Kate Pearce

Raven roared with laughter. "More trouble, Olaf? We have the king's son. Another hostage will simply double our advantage." He pinched Thea's nipple and only narrowly avoided her kick to his shins. "I've always wanted to fuck an alien."

Sven knocked on Thea's bedroom door, his smile firmly in place. The king had just informed him that the Council was preparing to address the matter of dissolving his vow of servitude to the queen. He couldn't wait to tell Thea that he was finally a free man. His cock hardened as he thought of the celebration they could have. He pictured her welcoming him between her thighs, her thick cream as he slid inward, her gasps of pleasure when he pounded into her again and again.

His smile died as he took in the empty bed. Where had she gone? She wasn't due to meet with the security team until dinnertime. A growing noise registered in his ears and he swung back toward the door. He started to run as he realized the uproar came from the king and queen's apartments.

Harlan staggered down the stairs, blood streaming from his temple, his complexion gray. Sven grabbed hold of him and propped him up against the stairs. Around them chaos threatened as servants and soldiers milled around shouting and crying.

"Harlan, what happened?"

"Someone took the young prince."

"What?" Sven clutched at Harlan's tunic. "How in Odin's name did that come to pass?"

"It was a woman, she attacked me from behind and knocked me out." Harlan swallowed hard. "It was my fault. I thought she was the prince's usual nursemaid. She wore her garments. I didn't think to question her being there."

Sven patted his shoulder, his mind working furiously through the various options.

"Where are the king and queen?"

168

"They went out riding with Bron and some of the others."

"Get someone to clean up that blow to your head and then concentrate on letting the king know what happened."

"What will you be doing?"

Sven smiled grimly. "I'll be checking the concealed cameras Thea insisted we had installed in the palace hallways so that I can see exactly what is going on." He turned toward the stairwell and Harlan grabbed his sleeve.

"I'm sorry, Sven. You don't think they'll harm the child do you?"

"I doubt it. This is probably all about money or power."

Harlan nodded, his expression more purposeful. "I'll make sure I tell the king before anyone else does."

Sven ran back to the security center in the center of the palace. By Thor, he hoped he was right and that the cameras had captured the intruders on film. He watched intently, noting how little time elapsed after the woman first entered the suite and returned carrying the prince. He stiffened as Thea's image appeared on the stairs and challenged the woman. Wincing, he watched her fall. She must have hurt herself on the steps, but she didn't let it deter her from chasing right after the woman. Part of him raged that she hadn't waited for backup; the hunter in him recognized her instinctive urge to go after the thieves.

He watched a while longer, half-hoping to see Thea reappear. A sick feeling grew in his belly. Had the gang taken her as well? He knew from bitter personal experience what happened to women who were stolen. They were used for sex by any man in the settlement and forced to breed until they died of it.

Despite Marcus' best efforts there were still males on the planet who wanted to hold to the old ways of stealing women and children rather than settling down and trying to produce their own. Sven rewound the tape and stared at Thea's frozen image on the screen. He couldn't let another woman suffer like his wife had. He noted the passageway Thea had disappeared down and got to his feet. Time was on his side. The kidnappers were unlikely to suspect one man would come after them, especially when the king's son was involved. Perhaps the element of surprise would work in his favor.

He quickly assembled his weapons and enough rations and water to see him through the next forty-eight hours and went to find Harlan. His fellow bodyguard stood on guard in front of the king's empty suite, keeping out the curious and the rest of the palace staff. His head was bandaged but he still looked pale.

He nodded when he saw Sven and then winced. "I've sent a message to the king. I'll await his return." He gestured at Sven's pack. "Are you going to take them out alone?"

"I'm going to try."

"Good luck. I'll tell the king. We'll make sure to follow through on any contact or negotiations on a bigger scale to buy you some time."

Sven took the stairway Thea had used and followed it right to the bottom. As he approached the hollowed-out storage bay, he caught the distinctive smell of blood in the fetid air. He stopped and studied a bundle of clothes on the dirt floor. Was that Thea? He went forward, crouched down to poke the pile and heaved a shuddering sigh of relief. His fingers trembled as he wiped them on his thigh. Nay, just the discarded robes the woman had borrowed from one of the palace servants.

He stood up, circled the cavern and noted how many pairs of feet had trampled the sand. He reckoned there were at least five of them, if not six. He walked across to the narrow mouth of the cave on the far side of the hollowed out space and smelled brackish water. Had they followed the narrow tunnels formed by one of the underground rivers? Thea had warned them that these waterways might be a security risk.

A small mark in vivid red caught his attention. He crouched down to look at it. Someone had marked a crude arrow in the direction of the tunnels. He straightened as hope flooded through him. Thea was definitely with them and was trying to help him track her. The only down side was that he had to assume she'd made the mark with her own blood.

Thea hated enclosed spaces. Hell, she'd tried to pretend she didn't care about them during training exercises with the police and security forces on Earth. She'd suffered in silence and dealt with the nightmares afterward alone and in private. But she still didn't like them. And here she was, traveling with a band of kidnappers through a rapidly narrowing series of tunnels beneath the immense weight of the Valhallan palace.

The stench of spoiled water was bad enough, but combined with the sweat pouring off the unwashed men around her it was enough to make her retch. She kept moving, her gaze on the little prince who seemed to be sleeping peacefully in the woman's arms. Had they drugged him? She frowned and hoped they hadn't overdone it.

Somebody was bound to notice the king's son and heir was missing pretty soon. She imagined what Sven would do when he found her and the baby gone. Would he come after her? She sure hoped so. With a choked cry, she pretended to stumble and came down on one knee. The knife she'd liberated from her first downed opponent was stuffed down the side of her boot and made her fall more awkwardly than she'd intended. Before she was pulled to her feet, she scratched at the cut on her throat, allowed a drop of blood to stain her fingertips and smudged it onto the nearest rock.

"Get up, woman."

She cried out as she was viciously hauled to her feet by the man called Raven. She cowered away as he lifted a hand to her. She hated to appear weak in front of him, but it was essential that he began to think of her as no threat.

"Don't hurt me, please."

He roared with laughter. "Earth women are obviously weaklings compared to our females. Maya here doesn't beg until she's been fucked by at least five men and knows there are more to come."

Maya didn't answer him, her attention fixed on the baby she carried and the rocky path ahead of her. Thea allowed herself to be pushed along the passageway, fighting the instinct to shove at the ever encroaching walls and scream to be set free. The ceiling lowered until they all had to crouch. She started crawling, her hands scraping on bare rock. God, Sven had to find her.

The sunlight hurt Thea's eyes, but she headed for it anyway, the faint gleam of an escape from the underground river worth every torturous movement toward it. She slithered through the hacked out hole in the rock and collapsed onto warm purple sand. Rolling onto her back she sucked in great drafts of the warm air. A *wulfran* neighed in alarm and kicked sand into her face. Raven pulled her to her feet.

"Come on, woman. We still have a long way to travel. "

She tried to scrape some blood from her throat onto the sheer rock wall behind her. The cut had dried up and she resigned herself to more pain. She pivoted and tried to claw at Raven's face like a girl would, using her nails and screaming at the top of her voice. He laughed as he backhanded her and she fell against the rocks leaving a fresh trail of blood from her busted lip on the surface. It took all her strength to stand up and move away from the incriminating marks. Sven had better see them and hurry up because either she'd run out of blood soon or be beaten to a pulp.

Sven frowned at yet more evidence of a bloody encounter on the scattering of rocks in front of him. A mess of footprints and the tracks of one lame *wulfran* were all that remained to mark the kidnapper's flight. What was Thea trying to do? Get herself killed? She probably had no idea how close he was behind her. Not that he didn't appreciate the clues she'd left him, they'd certainly made his task of tracking the marauders a whole lot easier. He just wished she hadn't endangered herself to help him. With a curse, he wiped the sticky residue of blood off on his leather pants, a sick feeling still in his gut.

From his vantage point on the ridge of one of the low hills, he shaded his eyes and focused on the small pinprick figures on the desert sand ahead of him. He estimated, they were only an Earth hour or less ahead of him now. He'd been able to contact the palace stables and provide himself with the king's best *wulfran*. The robbers had two women, an ancient *wulfran* and a baby to slow them down.

Sven checked his weapons and clicked to the *wulfran*. The suns would be setting in an hour or two, and he wanted to make sure he was close enough to see if the robber band decided to camp for the night or push on. He smiled grimly as he mounted the *wulfran*. Whatever happened, Thea and the young prince would no longer be with them by morning.

"Can we stop soon?"

Thea tried to sound as weak as possible. For the last hour she'd been sitting behind Raven on his decrepit *wulfran*, leaning as much of her weight on him as she could. He smelled like distilled yak but she had no choice. Baby Thor had started wailing a while ago, the sound rising and rising as he realized he wasn't with his mother. His cries tore at Thea's heart. She wanted to hold the little prince in her arms, rock him and tell him everything would be okay.

"We'll stop when I say so."

To her secret delight, Raven sounded as rattled as she felt, his gaze endlessly sweeping the vast empty purple horizon, his mouth pinched.

"There's shelter up ahead on the left, Raven."

Olaf, one of the other men pointed to a shadowed bank of hills surrounded by rocky outcrops.

"All right, we'll stop." Raven cast a furious glance at the nursemaid. "And if you don't stop that brat crying I'll cut out his tongue."

Thea tried to find some solace in the fact that Raven hadn't threatened to kill the baby but it didn't help much. She hurried over to Maya as soon as she got off the *wulfran.*

"Is there anything I can do to help?"

Maya glanced at her, her eyes wide with fear.

"Nay, my lady. I have milk to feed the babe. He'll quieten down then."

"I hope you're right for all our sakes," Thea muttered. She yelped as Raven yanked her back toward him by her hair. His wet mouth closed on her throat and sucked greedily. She forced herself to go limp in his grasp.

"When we've all settled down for the night, you'd better be ready to get properly fucked, Earth woman. We'll take it in turns to see who can make you beg and plead the loudest." He bit her neck. "I bet it will be me."

He shoved her away and she hit the ground, banging her shoulder against the rocks. She curled up in a ball and kept still until he turned away with a satisfied grunt. God, he was *so* going to die. She'd never been particularly bloodthirsty but he deserved everything she intended to do to him. She touched the knife in her boot and focused her gaze on the hills that led back to the palace. Sven was out there somewhere, she just knew it. If all went according to plan, she'd soon be joining him and returning to the luxurious surroundings of the king's palace.

After a lot of grumbling, two of the men disappeared out toward the reaches of their camp to act as guards. Baby Thor had gone back to sleep and Raven remained with Olaf and the two women. Maya had bedded down with the baby in the sheltered entrance to one of the larger caves. Thea's ankles were tied but her hands were left free to eat the meager dried rations Maya gave her. She listened carefully as Raven and Olaf talked through their plans to ransom the young prince. It became apparent that Olaf was the one with a brain and that Raven was simply a bully who got his way through intimidation and fear.

It seemed the plan was for them to journey on another day to the band's more secure hideout and then send Olaf back with a ransom demand to the king. Thea wanted to laugh out loud and tell them what a bunch of amateurs they were. Unfortunately it didn't fit in with her cowed female impersonation. If her plan was to work, she needed them to believe she was useless and weak.

Finally Raven belched loudly and stood up, his gaze resting on Thea who pretended to sleep against a pile of rocks. While Raven was boasting to Maya she'd used her stolen knife to cut through the rope around her ankles and was more than ready for him.

"Olaf, go and check on Maya and the baby."

Olaf stood too, his uneasy gaze shifting between his boss and Thea.

"Are you sure you want to be alone with her, Raven? She's an alien. She might be dangerous."

"Dangerous?" Raven laughed. "She's done nothing but complain and moan the whole time. A few weeks spent servicing our war band will probably kill her!" he gestured at Olaf. "Go and check on Maya. I'll give this alien female a quick fuck, show her whose in charge, and then let you have a turn, all right?"

"All right. I'll be back in a few minutes."

Thea watched as Raven's boots came closer and closer. He knelt down in front of her, one hand fumbling with the buttons of his fly. He slapped her cheek until she opened her eyes.

175

"Take my cock in your mouth, bitch."

While Raven shoved down his pants and struggled to release his erection, Thea slid her hand down to find her knife. By the time he grasped her head and tried to shove his cock into her mouth, she had the knife positioned at his balls. He jumped as cold steel grazed his tender flesh.

"Now let go of me, you bastard," Thea hissed, "Or I'll slice off your balls."

Raven's punishing grip on her head relaxed and then disappeared. He made a sudden lunge for the knife, but Thea was ready for him. She rolled to one side, came up onto the balls of her feet and delivered three quick fast kicks to his jawbone. He dropped like a stone, his head hitting the ground with a deeply satisfying thud. While he was unconscious, Thea stripped him of weapons, used the rope to bind his feet and hands and gagged him.

When she turned back to the cave entrance she found Olaf and Maya staring at her. She advanced toward them, knife at the ready.

"If you want the king to be lenient, let me take the child back with me. I will personally tell the king that you helped me escape and you will avoid death."

Maya looked up at Olaf, her expression confused and terrified. Olaf sighed.

"I told Raven it was a stupid plan, but he refused to listen to me. He was desperate for money to buy land in the newly fertile valleys."

"Land to farm?"

"Nay, for a war camp to prey on anyone who tried to make a living there."

Thea looked back at Raven who was starting to twitch and murmur. "Then he doesn't deserve your loyalty. If you help me, I'll ask the king to make you a land grant to use properly."

Hope flickered in Olaf's eyes and he took Maya's hand.

"Perhaps you could tie us up and make it look as if we were captured as well."

Thea smiled through the pain of her throbbing headache. "Done."

With a feral smile, Sven crept up on the guard, who was too busy taking a piss to notice anything around him, and locked his arm around the man's neck. The guard jerked backward, almost tearing Sven's arm off. He went quiet as Sven pricked his throat with his dagger.

"Where are the females?"

The man muttered a curse. Sven tightened his grip and let the blade cut a little deeper.

"Where are they?"

He sensed danger behind him and shoved the first guard away. He turned but it was too late. A crushing blow to his skull took him to the ground and he knew no more.

Thea checked Raven one last time and found him still unconscious. If it was up to her, she hoped he stayed that way. She'd borrowed Maya's cloak and the sling used to transport the baby and had Thor strapped firmly across her chest. Who would've guessed that a small baby would weigh so much? He was obviously made of pure muscle just like his father. She nodded at Maya and Olaf who were trussed up like chickens at the entrance to the cave.

She took a deep breath. All she had to do now was avoid the two other guys, persuade Raven's ancient *wulfran* to move faster than a shuffle and get back to the palace. "Piece of cake", as her British martial arts coach would've said, whatever that meant. She stared down into baby Thor's big golden eyes. He looked disconcertingly like King Marcus.

"If you want to get home, you'll have to be a good boy, okay? No screaming or crying."

He blinked back at her as if he totally understood.

"Okay, then we'll be off."

She covered him over with the edges of her cloak and managed to grab the *wulfran's* reins. The guards would be back soon, hoping for another bite to eat or a turn in the sack with her. Thea shivered. If she could avoid them, she would. If not, she'd have to think of something fast. She started to pick her way through the ragged boulders toward the desert and the hills they'd passed through earlier. Thank god she had a great sense of direction. Was Sven out there somewhere, waiting for a chance to help her out? She sure hoped so.

The first guard wasn't where he was supposed to be. Thea stopped moving and crouched in the shadow of a cave entrance. She could hear voices to her left where the purple desert sand dipped down to form a small hollow.

Had they spotted Sven? Was that what the excitement was about? She picked up a large rock, tucked her cloak more firmly around her and crawled toward the lip of the hollow. Below her stood the two guards. One of them was bleeding, the other was busy tying up another man who lay motionless on the ground. Thea squinted against the fading light. The guard stood up and landed a kick on the man's ribs. A shock of red hair caught the dying rays of the sun.

Thea closed her eyes as a wave of horror rolled over her. It seemed that her back up plan had run into trouble.

"Thor's Bones," Sven muttered through his chapped lips. "What happened?"

"Shut up, cur."

Sven grunted as someone kicked him. His cheek was plastered against the burning desert sand, his hands locked together at the small of his back. By Odin, he remembered now. He'd tried to intercept one of the guards and been hit hard on the back of the head. He blinked slowly as his vision blurred and his stomach rolled. He was a fool, an idiot, a conceited coward. What hope for Thea now that he had failed her?

"What shall we do with him, then?"

The voice was young and anxious.

"We'll take him back to Raven. He can decide."

"Do you think we can carry him? He's huge."

Another kick landed on Sven's back.

"We'll tie him behind the *wulfran* and drag him."

Sven closed his eyes as the men's shadows moved away from him. His head hurt. He had to try to focus. If they took him back to the camp where they were holding Thea and the baby, he still stood a chance.

"Excuse me?"

Sven stiffened. God's, he must be hallucinating. That sounded just like Thea. He rolled onto his back and tried to concentrate. A narrow figure stood at the top of the hill, cloak billowing in the gathering breeze. The smaller of the two men took a step forward.

"What are you doing here, alien bitch? You're supposed to be tied up!"

"Raven sent me."

Sven strained to hear her soft reply, only aware that the two men were leaving him to go after her. He struggled to right himself, managed to get one knee under him before he had to stop and wait for the world to right itself.

The smaller man had reached her now. Sven gritted his teeth. He couldn't get to her in time, he couldn't save her. Thea leaned toward the bastard, her smile inviting.

To Sven's amazement, the man collapsed on the ground and slowly rolled back down the hill coming to rest beside Sven in an untidy heap.

"Hey! What did you do to him?"

Sven checked the man's face. What had she done? There was a rapidly growing bump on the man's forehead. Whatever she'd hit him with must've hurt. Sven managed to stagger to his feet just as the bigger guy grabbed Thea's shoulder. With a roar of rage, Sven forced himself to move forward in the shifting sand. He kept his weight low and head-butted the man in the back before falling face first into the sand on top of his opponent.

"Good job, Sven. You looked just like one of those NFL players."

Sven groaned, tried to raise his head and failed. Thea's feet disappeared and he concentrated on breathing and mastering the urge to retch.

After a little while, he managed to half roll onto his side. Thea crouched beside the bigger man, her hands busy.

"Where is the prince?" Sven managed to croak.

Thea didn't turn away from her still unconscious captive. "He's right here, under my cloak. He's been such a good boy."

Sven swallowed hard as an unaccustomed urge to weep filled him. He blinked rapidly as Thea's concerned face swam over him.

"Are you okay, Sven?"

"I have failed you, my lady."

She frowned. "What?"

"I am a useless man."

She sighed. "Sven, could you take a rain check on the emotional crisis and just get up and help me drag these guys back to their camp?"

"Aye, my lady."

He nodded abruptly and winced with pain. It was obvious that she was too disgusted with his unmanly actions to even talk to him. He drew his legs up under him and managed to get to his knees. At least he could salvage some pride and obey her orders. Despite his concussion, he was still capable of lifting the two dolts and putting them wherever she wanted.

By the time she and Sven returned the two guards to the camp, the suns were setting and a dark purple haze crept across the desert. Thea glanced at Sven as he moved slowly around the rocks looking for fuel for the dying fire. His face was set, his complexion gray. She sure hoped he was okay. He'd hardly said a word to her, let alone given her the hug she so badly needed.

She turned back to survey the desert and caught her breath. Lights were approaching from the direction of the city. Were they about to be rescued or were there more members of Raven's gang of thieves?

"Sven, do you see that?"

He came up behind her.

"Aye. We should take shelter in the cave until we know whether they are friend or foe. I left some signs for the King to follow, but we cannot take any chances with the young prince."

Thea glanced down at baby Thor. He was still sleeping, apparently unaffected by the high drama going on around him. Great. Obviously Sven thought *her* survival was not even worth a mention. Her bad mood intensified. All she'd done was save the prince and Sven and suddenly everything was her fault?

Without speaking, she turned abruptly on her heel and headed for the cave. Raven glared at her as she passed, his mouth moving beneath his gag. She smiled at him and he spluttered even more. She sure hoped it was the king. Meeting any more of Raven's pals was not high on her to-do list.

Thea shivered as the coolness of the cave settled over her. Sven came to stand in front of her, one hand barring her exit, head turned toward the rapidly approaching lights. A shrill whistle pierced the air and he stiffened. Thea jumped as he returned the call. The sound echoed around the cave, waking Thor who started to fuss at Thea's breast.

"It is the king."

Thea glared up at Sven. "I sure hope so, now that you've woken the baby. Let's hope the queen is with him too so that she can feed the little blighter."

Sven leaned back against the cave wall as Marcus took his son gently into his arms. The stark emotion on the king's face barely penetrated Sven's exhaustion. He should be down on his knees thanking the gods for his king's happiness, but he felt numb. He'd done nothing to rescue either the woman he loved or the king's child.

Thea walked toward him and he straightened. She smiled up at him.

"Thank you for saving me."

He averted his gaze. "There is no need to be cruel, my lady."

"What?"

"I did nothing. I failed you as I failed my first wife. When she was abducted, I couldn't save her either. She died in my arms giving birth to my son."

"God, I'm sorry, Sven." Her face softened and she touched his shoulder. "But I meant what I said. You did help me."

He snorted. "I left you to fend for yourself. You were the one who was the hero, not me."

She put her hands on her hips. "I did what needed to be done and so did you. Does it really matter who saved who?"

"It does to me."

"Why? Because you have to be the hero and you didn't think I was capable?"

His smile was as bitter as the taste of failure in his mouth. "You are more than capable, my lady. You don't need my help at all."

Tears glinted in her eyes as she glared at him. "Did it occur to you that the only thing that kept me going, was the thought that you would come after me? Everything I did was with that knowledge, that you would find me whatever happened."

He held her gaze. "But I didn't find you. You found me."

She stepped back, her voice low, her breathing ragged. "Sven...don't do this. Don't fight with me when all I need is to feel your arms around me, telling me that everything will be okay."

He clenched his hands into fists in an effort not to reach for her.

"I'm not worthy to touch you, my lady. It seems I'm incapable of protecting those I love."

She wrapped her arms around her waist as if giving herself the comfort he denied her. "If you truly love me, you won't do this."

He stared at her, his gut tightening. "Nay, you deserve better. I can't risk seeing you hurt again."

Her smile was bitter sweet. "But didn't you just admit that I can protect myself?" She took another step back. "That's the real problem isn't it, Sven? Why can't you let me take care of myself and worry about your own safety?"

"Because that is not the Valhallan way."

"And that worked out so well for you last time, didn't it? Because *the Valhallan way* meant your wife wasn't trained to defend herself and she died."

He took a step toward her, anger shuddering through him, his voice echoed through the cave. "She died because I couldn't protect her!"

Thea swallowed hard. "She died because of the Valhallan way of life. It wasn't your fault."

Sven bowed. "It doesn't matter what you say. I know who is at fault."

"And you're going to let your past mistakes dictate your future?"

Sven closed his eyes as a wave of dizziness washed over him. "I am going to set you free to find a man who is worthy of you."

"Fine!" Thea glared at him, her chin high in the air. "You just do that, Sven Magnusson. If you want to live in the past, go right ahead, you stupid ox."

She turned her back on him and pushed her way through the crowd of soldiers surrounding the king. Sven let out his breath and focused on a familiar face. Bron stood watching him, his expression concerned.

"Did you hear all that?" Sven said.

Bron nodded. "I think everyone did."

Sven pushed away from the rock and headed back toward the tethered *wulfran.* Now all he had to do was get on the damn beast and leave before he added to his disgrace and shed unmanly tears. "Good, now perhaps you'll *all* leave me alone."

Thea allowed herself to be fussed over and thanked by the queen and king until she could barely keep awake. Sven had disappeared. She hoped he'd gotten some treatment for his head, but she suspected he was simply avoiding her.

"I think Ms. Cooper needs her sleep."

The king's amused voice cut through the queen's last question.

"Of course, Marcus, you're right," Douglass said as she patted Thea's hand. "I just wanted to thank her."

The king stood up and bowed. "I think you did that, my love, about a thousand times. Let me escort you back to bed, Ms. Cooper."

Thea walked along the quiet marble halls beside the king, his bare feet made no sound of the polished floors. The few people they encountered bowed low and smiled at Thea as if she had given them an unexpected gift. Strange to find herself a heroine on a planet that believed its women should be sequestered and not taught how to fight. Perhaps her exploits, along with the queen's radical plans would begin to change that misconception.

The king held open the door to her suite and followed her inside. Thea forced herself to smile up at him.

"Thank you. I think I can take it from here."

She jumped when the king took her hand and went down on one knee in front of her. His gesture as elegant and smooth as a powerful cat. He kissed her fingers one by one.

"I am in your debt, Thea Cooper. If there is anything I can provide for you, just ask and I will do everything in my power to grant your request."

Thea sighed. "I don't suppose you know how to make an intergalactic Viking realize he is a fool?"

The king smiled slowly up at her.

"Actually I think I do."

Chapter Eleven

🙷

"You are a fool."

Harlan's face floated above Sven, his expression uncharacteristically grim.

Sven swallowed hard and managed to sit up. At least he was in his own bed again and not back in the nightmarish desert of his dreams endlessly watching Thea walk away from him.

"What in Thor's name are you talking about?"

"This came from the king's council this morning for you."

Harlan tossed a roll of parchment at Sven and then leaned back against the wall, arms folded over his bare chest.

Sven unrolled the parchment and tried to focus on the elaborate Valhallan script. His head pounded as if a herd of *wulfran* had run over it. The healer had told him to expect a headache for a few days but no other lasting effects from the blow to his head.

He finished reading and let the document fall onto the sheets and roll back up.

"The Council has freed me from my vows to the king and queen. I am no longer obliged to be the queen's pleasure server."

"Aye."

Sven took a slow careful breath. "So now I have no job."

"You're still part of the security team. That is, if Ms. Cooper lets you stay on."

"What the hell is that supposed to mean?"

Harlan raised an eyebrow.

"Didn't you know? Ms. Cooper was confirmed by the king as the new head of Valhallan security today."

"But that's my job."

"Not any more." Harlan levered himself away from the wall. "You, my friend, are in a lot of trouble."

"Harlan."

Sven tensed as Harlan paused by the door.

"What am I supposed to do?"

"About what?"

"About, all this…" Sven touched the parchment on the bed. "Two days ago this news would've made me the happiest man alive. Now I have nothing."

"And you expect me to feel sorry for you?"

Sven glared at him and started to get up. "Aye, unless you would take a woman's side against one of your oldest friends."

Harlan half-turned back toward the door. "As I said, you're a fool. To throw away your chance at happiness because of hurt pride is unforgivable."

"Is that what she's telling everyone?"

"Ms. Cooper isn't saying anything. She just walks around looking as if someone has stolen her joy. I heard what you said to her at the caves, Sven. Everyone did."

"You think I do this out of inflated pride?"

Harlan held his gaze. "It would be just like you to feel belittled because a female saved you."

"It's not that."

"Then what? What in Thor's name keeps you from claiming her?"

Sven sank back down onto the side of the bed and stared at his bare feet. "I can't risk it."

"Can't risk what?"

"Loving someone and losing them again."

Harlan sighed. "Sven, your wife died sixteen years ago when you were barely old enough to marry. You've grown up, you're not the same man. You wouldn't make the same mistakes again. Do you really want to spend the rest of your life mourning that loss?"

Sven said nothing and continued to stare at his feet, noticed the roughened and blistered skin from his frantic journey through the desert sands.

Harlan cleared his throat. "Not a fool then, but a coward."

Sven raised his head and scowled. "I am no coward."

"Aye, you are, but don't worry about it, Sven. I'm sure you're right, and a better man will come along and take Thea to wife. In fact, I'm going to seek her out now and see if I can bring a smile to her face."

Sven forced the words out. "Then I wish you luck. She would be well suited to you."

"Nay, she's well suited to you, but if you don't want her…"

Harlan left, slamming the door behind him. Sven continued to study the intricate tiled floor. Thea did deserve a better man than him. The trouble was, the thought of her touching another man made him physically sick. He closed his eyes and remembered the scent of her hair and the soft moans of pleasure she made when he slid inside her. Could he bear to stay on Valhalla and watch her try out potential mates without killing someone?

Nay. And if she'd accepted the job as security chief it didn't look as if she intended to return to Earth soon either. Could he live there instead? He glanced out the small window, caught the purple shimmer of the desert. He couldn't leave the beloved homeland that had just been restored to him.

With a resigned sigh, Sven got up and headed for the shower. For the first time in almost fifteen years, he had no idea what he was supposed to be doing. His job as the queen's pleasure server was gone as was his position as head of

Valhallan security. The only thing left to do was meet with Thea and see if she was prepared to let him work for her. He smiled bitterly. Perhaps she would enjoy ordering him about, as was her right. Perhaps he deserved to see her take another mate. It was a fitting punishment for a man with no honor or ability to protect his womenfolk.

Thea sighed as yet another tall Valhallan loomed over her. She'd taken over Sven's desk in the security office and buried herself in work. Making the palace more secure was now her top priority. Since Sven's public rejection of her, every Valhallan male in the palace had found an excuse to come by and "chat". Not that they weren't pleasant and great eye candy, but the only person she really wanted to see was Sven.

The king's plan to bring Sven around had shocked and aroused Thea, but she still wasn't sure if she'd get the opportunity to try it out.

When the king had offered her the position as head of Valhallan security, she was uncertain what to do. It had never been her intention to take Sven's job away from him. The king insisted her acceptance was vital to the success of the plan and Thea reluctantly agreed.

"My lady?"

She finally looked up. It was Harlan, his expression warm, his eyes full of concern.

"What's up?"

"Sven wishes to talk to you."

She managed a shrug. "What's stopping him? My door is open."

"Perhaps he thought you might not wish to see him."

Thea tried a smile. "Why would he think that? It's not like I don't get dumped in front of an audience every day."

Harlan winked and lowered his voice. "If you need Bron and me to get him down to the caverns, let me know."

"It depends how this discussion goes."

"Good luck, then."

Thea took a deep breath as Sven appeared at the door. To her secret relief, he looked as tired and strained as she felt. She gestured to the chair in front of her desk.

"Sit down, Mr. Magnusson. What can I do for you?"

He sat, his gaze fixed on his linked hands.

"I am wondering if you have a job for me."

Thea winced at his humble tone. This wasn't the Sven she'd imagined coming into the office, roaring at her, demanding his job back, taking her hard on the desk...

"A job? Don't you already have one with the queen?"

He shrugged. "Nay. The Council has freed me from my vows."

Thea waited to see if he had anything else to say. Anything else suggesting he was free to claim her and would she accept his heart? He continued to stare down at his hands. Thea barely controlled an urge to slap him.

"Great! Now you can go and find some meek little Valhallan woman to keep safe forever."

To her dismay, Sven didn't even react.

"I would like a job."

She stared at him. "Do you really think you'd be able to work for me? Do what I say and not argue?"

He shrugged. "If it is the only way for me to remain in the palace, then yes."

Thea stood up. "I don't believe you."

Sven rose too, his expression darkening. Anticipation curled in Thea's stomach.

"You have taken my job. Do you want to steal my home from me as well?"

"What the hell is that supposed to mean?"

He shrugged. "If I don't work in the palace, I have no right to be here."

Thea raised her eyebrows. "Do you expect me to feel sorry for you? You made your choices."

Sven braced his palms on the edge of the desk. "Aye, I did. What do I have to do to prove I am serious, kiss your feet?"

"Maybe it's time to find out."

Thea smiled slowly and walked past Sven to the door. Bron and Harlan were waiting in the hallway.

"Take Sven down to the temple and contact Woden. I'm sure he won't want to miss this."

Sven allowed himself to be led down to the lower levels of the palace without complaint. He had no idea what Thea was up to, but he wasn't prepared to fight yet.

"Bring him in here."

That was the king's voice. Sven hesitated as Bron guided him through a carved arched doorway into the ancient palace temple. He'd never been in this most sacred of female Valhallan places before. Water flowed from a circular fountain set to one side. Oil lamps and torches illuminated the cavernous rose-colored space. The crumbling marble walls were painted with intricate patterns worshipping the union of male and female and the promise of fertility.

The king stood in the center of the room, arms folded across his naked chest, Woden right behind him.

"Bring him to me."

Sven faced his king, noticed the lack of amusement on his face. A trickle of unease spread through his gut.

"Take off your clothes, Sven."

"Why?"

Marcus raised his eyebrows. "I am your king. I do not have to answer your questions."

191

Sven obliged, glad that the warmth of the underground chamber hid his shivering. He straightened to find the king had moved to one side, revealing the stone structure behind him.

"Stand by the rack."

"The rack?" Sven stared at the king. "Are you punishing me for leaving your wife's service? I thought you agreed…"

"Be silent." Marcus moved to stand by the stones. "Come here."

Sven took a deep breath. If this was some ritual punishment for breaking his vows to the queen then perhaps it was best to simply get it over with. But what did this have to do with Thea? He approached the king and waited for his next instruction.

"Get his wrists."

Harlan and Bron stepped up beside him and enclosed his wrists in silver manacles that looked as old as the room. After another command from the king, they moved him to stand between the stone posts.

"Use the steps cut in the stone to climb up to the platform and kneel."

Sven counted the rough, well-used steps. There were only about five, bringing the level of the structure up to his waist height. He used the footholds to ascend and knelt on the worn stone platform, his knees fitting easily into the grooves. Harlan and Bron each grasped one of his wrists and drew them over his head, attaching the manacles to a chain above him. His arms were stretched tight, his muscles stretching against the slight strain.

He stiffened when they grabbed his ankles and manacled them to the stone as well. The king walked around to face him.

"In the ancient days of Valhallan culture, the female ruled. The queen and priestesses used to bring their mates here to remind them of their duties."

Sven stared at the king. *What in Thor's name was he on about?* Marcus inclined his head.

"You may speak."

"I don't understand. My duty to what? To you and the queen?"

"Nay, your duty to your woman."

Sven licked his dry lips. "I have no woman."

"I believe you do and she intends to remind you of your responsibilities. Perhaps you need to learn that being subservient to your soul mate is all about trust."

"You would let the queen do this to you?"

Marcus smiled. "She already has." His smile faded and he nodded at Woden. "Oil him."

Sven refused to look at any of his companions as Woden spread oil over his chest and back. He flinched as Woden's hands slid lower to cover his buttocks, his balls and his cock. Sensation flooded through him as the orange-scented oil heated on his skin and his shaft stirred. The king spoke again.

"Put on his cock ring."

Harlan stepped forward, his expression calm and grasped Sven's cock. With a few practiced movements he had Sven half-erect and slid the thick metal ring down over his shaft and tightened it.

"Are you ready, My Queen?"

"Yes, Sire."

Sven's gaze jerked to the right as the queen appeared, clad only in jeweled rubies and thick gold chains, her long dark hair flowing down her back. She approached Sven and stood in front of him. He held his breath as she stared at his rapidly expanding rod.

"Make him hard."

The queen bent forward, her breasts swinging slightly and took his cock in her mouth. Sven tried not to speak as the metal ring bit into his swelling shaft. He arched to angle his hips into the rhythm set by the queen's mouth but he couldn't move. A groan burst from his mouth as his balls clenched and drew closer to his body.

"Gag him, Bron."

Before Sven could utter a protest, Bron was behind him, expertly shoving a ball gag into his mouth and tying the leather behind his head. The king stepped forward, two clamps in his hands and applied them to Sven's aching nipples. Sven began to pant, the overload of sensations driving him wild. He was so close to coming, his focus on the queen's red lips as they moved over his cock, the hollowing of her cheeks and the ruby red flash of her jewels as she bent toward him.

"Stop, My Queen."

Sven wanted to scream when the queen withdrew her mouth, leaving his hot, wet cock exposed to the suddenly cold air. His shaft jerked upward, seeking the pleasure to be found in her mouth, desperate to come.

He struggled to look up as the queen went to stand by the king.

"Well done, My Queen." Marcus made a low sound of approval as his fingers traced Douglass' breast, found her nipple and squeezed. "Now we leave him for his female to decide his fate."

He bowed in Sven's direction.

"I suggest you think very carefully about your choices, Sven. This is your last opportunity to prove to your woman that you are eager to serve her properly and that you are prepared to humble yourself before her to earn her love."

He took the queen's hand and turned away. Sven stared after the other bodyguards as they followed the king out of the underground temple. Silence fell, broken only by the tinkling water and the faint echoes of movement above.

What in the god's name was he supposed to do now? Wait for Thea to come and untie him? Would she even want to? She'd already saved his ass once this week. He tried to shift his weight, aware of the worn stone beneath his knees and the pulse thundering through his painfully erect cock. If she had any sense she'd simply laugh at him and walk away.

Time slid by, measured by each of his labored breaths and each heated throb of his trapped shaft. Sven remained hard and ready, the cock ring preventing his release. By Odin, he wanted her to come for him, so that he could shove his cock deep inside her until he gained his release and then start again until she screamed his name to the heavens. He wanted her — whatever she thought of him. A sliver of hope formed in his chest. By prostrating himself like this, by showing her that he could be bound and helpless and accept her domination, would she take him back?

He breathed out hard through his nose. By Thor, he hoped so. If the king could survive such exquisite sexual torture for the sake of his wife, Sven could to. He raised his head as a slight movement of perfumed air stirred his already overwrought senses. Thea stood by the doorway, her gaze fixed on his body.

Oh my God.

Thea stared at Sven's gleaming oiled torso. His wrists were shackled above his head displaying the taut muscles of his arms and his exquisite abs. She licked her lips, aware that she yearned to suck every perfumed inch of his skin until he begged for mercy. His cock stood high and proud away from his stomach, the thick gleam of pre-cum catching the lamplight.

She took her time circling him, saw the silver manacles around his ankles and the tight curve of his hip and buttocks. Strange to have him displayed for her like this, his strong voice silenced, his strength and movement restricted. She reached out to stroke his ass and his whole body quivered.

Damn, she sure hoped the king was right about this. He'd told her exactly what she needed to do to bring Sven to his senses. Of course, if Sven didn't want her to see him helpless like this, she would lose him completely. But if he did? It was time for her to believe in herself and what she wanted rather than walking away. And oh, despite his earlier behavior, she wanted him bad. Taking all her courage in her hands, Thea walked back around to face Sven. His brown eyes followed her every move.

She moved closer, touched the jeweled nipple clamps and the thick metal of his cock ring, ran her fingers around the edge of the leather ball gag until he tried desperately to move toward her.

Slowly she removed her clothes, watching as his breathing altered and his cock grew even wetter. She picked up one of the sex toys the king and queen had left for her on the ancient altar. Sven's eyes widened as he registered what she held in her hand. She showed him the small leather butt plug.

"The king told me that in the olden days, part of this ceremony involved me fucking you with this. It was seen as a sign of complete trust and submission. Would you let me put it in you?"

She waited, her breath coming unevenly from her throat as he stared at her. All he had to do was shake his head and it was all over.

He bowed his head, the picture of humble submission. Thea felt her body respond with a welling of cream and a persistent throb in her clit. She slid the leather plug between her own legs and coated it in her juices.

The oil coating Sven's ass helped her lubricate him and slowly slide the leather butt plug home. He groaned deep in his throat as she moved it in and out of him, imitating a long, slow fuck. Eager to share his pleasure, she pressed her mound to the rounded end of the plug and circled her hips, enjoying the sensation on her already aroused clit. She slid one hand around his waist and played with the tip of his cock, sliding her finger in and out of the wet swollen slit until he bucked and writhed within his bonds.

It felt good to touch him like this. To make him hers, to brand him as her perfect lover. Perhaps the king had been right and Sven needed this even more than she did. His reaction to her touch left her in no doubt that he was enjoying the rough treatment, the restriction of his bonds and the ever-increasing ache of sexual arousal.

With that thought, Thea climaxed, her grip of Sven's cock dangerously tight as she moaned her delight. Leaving the butt plug in place she moved back around to the front. Sven's body was coated in a fine sheen of sweat making the perfume in the oil fill the air and mingle with the scent of her arousal. He was breathing hard as if he'd been running.

Thea smiled at him.

"I like you like this, Sven. All mine, to do whatever I want to." She studied his cock, licked at the steady flow of pre-cum. "Perhaps being trapped by a woman isn't quite as bad as you thought?"

He shook his head, his eyes fierce above the gag. Thea licked her lips.

"Perhaps it's good for you to realize that trusting me to take care of myself," she flicked his cock, "and of you, doesn't necessarily mean you aren't still a big, strong Valhallan male."

She reached up and took off the nipple clamps, kissed each nipple and sucked them until he shuddered.

"Perhaps you've come to realize that having a woman who can take care of herself—and you, might even be a good thing?" She stepped back and sat cross-legged on the ground in front of him. She touched her breasts, squeezed her nipples until she was moaning and then slid her hand down between her legs.

"I can even make myself come." She thumbed her clit, slipped three fingers into her wet, slippery channel and rocked into a familiar rhythm. She held Sven's gaze, aware that she was behaving outrageously, but not caring in the slightest. If this was what it would take to completely enslave him, then she'd give it all she had. He was worth it.

She climaxed hard, and he closed his eyes as if he couldn't bear to watch her enjoy herself without him. When she'd finished shuddering she got to her feet and wiped her wet hand over his tight abs. His nostrils flared as he inhaled her scent.

"Of course, it's much better if you join in, but I can manage in a crisis."

He nodded, his fierce concentration fixed on her face. She held his gaze.

"If I walked away now and left you unsatisfied, would you still be erect when I returned? Would you still want me?"

He nodded quickly, but she saw the flash of desperation in his eyes.

"Tomorrow?"

He swallowed hard, the muscles of his throat working convulsively and nodded again. She stared at him, realized he meant it, realized she had what she wanted within her grasp. With a sigh, she kissed the crown of his cock.

"I'll see you later then."

Despite his bonds, he made a stifled sound and a convulsive movement toward her before he stilled. She blew him a kiss and walked out into the darkened hallway beyond.

She'd left him.

She'd fucking walked away and left him with a raging hard-on and a plug up his ass. Sven stared at the open archway and willed her to come back. He needed to come more than he needed to breathe. Even his teeth ached in sympathy with his loaded balls. He stared down at his pulsing cock. Could he stay like this all night? Would she really do that to him?

He contemplated the water fountain which didn't help, reminding him as it did of gushing foam and wet bone-shaking completion. Could he make himself come? Experimentally he clenched his buttock muscles, felt the leather shift within him, moaned into the gag.

Possibly. But did he want to? Wasn't it a point of honor that he should still be here, erect and ready to service his woman whenever she demanded it? Thea had to realize that he was giving in to her and that he was prepared to see her as an equal rather than as a poor weak female who needed protecting. By Thor, if she took the gag off he'd tell her anything she wanted to hear!

His thoughts reverberated around his head. The king was right. His time in the temple had crystallized his intentions. There was no way that he was going to let another male, let alone a Valhallan male, take his woman. If she could accept him, pitiful male that he was, he could surely accept her. He frowned down at his cock. If he had to stay erect all night, he'd do it, if it brought Thea back to him.

"Shall I go back now?"

The king grinned at Thea.

"You've only been away from him for an hour. Don't you think he needs to suffer more?"

Thea bit her lip and pictured Sven's oiled body, the thick strength of his cock and the total turn-on of his complete submission to her. She got up from the couch and walked across to the window. The other bodyguards waited with the king, their relaxed presence reassuring and comforting. Outside, the two suns had set, leaving the palace bathed in the eerie purple light reflected from the desert.

"I've enjoyed making him suffer, but I'd kind of like to see it through to the end, now."

The king came to stand beside her, his expression sober. "You know what you have to do?" Thea nodded. "Then off you go."

Thea squeezed the king's massive biceps. "Thank you, Sire."

"You are more than welcome." The king bowed. "I hope you'll still believe that when you're stuck with Sven for the rest of your life."

She smiled at him even as her feet took her toward the door.

"If he gets too uppity, I'll just bring him back to the temple."

The king winked. "That's exactly what the queen says to me."

Thea found her way to the lower levels and paused in the hallway leading to the ancient temple. The only sound was the gushing of the ancient fountain and her breathing. Now came the tricky part. She had to unleash her tiger and see whether he intended to devour her or allow her to pet him a little more.

Sven looked up as she entered, his gaze alert, his cock stiff and ready for her. Despite her nerves, Thea gave him her most sensual smile.

"Are you still here?"

He blinked slowly, the only sign of his interest in the subtle tightening of his muscles.

"I'm glad you stayed around."

She walked behind him, took out the butt plug and dropped it to the floor. The silver manacles around his ankles came apart smoothly. Now came the difficult part. Thea used the stone steps to climb up to Sven's level and release his wrists. His groan of relief was audible even behind the gag. She got down as quickly as she could and guided him down to the marbled floor.

Before she could speak, he fell to his knees in front of her, head bowed, gaze on the floor. Thea tried to breathe and found it almost impossible as she contemplated his lithe form. Her fingers shook as she bent down to untie the gag and drew it away from his face. She touched his thick red hair, now damp with sweat, and pushed it away from his forehead. He still said nothing, his breathing as harried and uneven as hers.

"Do you acknowledge that I am your equal?"

He cleared his throat, his voice husky with misuse. "Aye, my lady. I was a fool."

She caught his face in her hands and stared into his brown eyes. "I'm quite capable of taking care of myself but that doesn't mean I don't want you or what you can offer me."

He swallowed hard. "My strength is your strength, my weakness your weakness. I understand that now. I even desire it."

She nodded slowly, realized she was crying when one of her tears hit his upturned face. With a moan of need, she kissed his mouth and outlined his lips with her tongue. His response was slow and careful as if he cherished every second of her touch.

"I am yours to command, my lady."

She knelt until she was level with him and reached for his cock. His breath hissed out as she wrapped her hand around his shaft.

"By Odin, my lady. I crave your touch more than I crave the air I breathe."

She studied his cock, bent her head and took the swollen crown into her mouth. His groan of relief echoed around the cavernous chamber as she moved her fingers in counterpoint to the pressure of her mouth. It took but a moment to have him coming hot and deep between her lips, each spurt sucked eagerly down her throat, each cry of completion music to her ears.

He collapsed against her, his whole body shivering and bucking as she swiftly removed his cock ring, his shaft continued to pulse in her palm as if eager for more. After a long moment, he took her hand and kissed it, his gaze serious and intent.

"I pledge you my life, Ms. Thea Cooper, my protection when you need it and I offer my love and support when you don't."

She covered his hand with hers. "And I offer you the same."

His rare smile transformed his face. "Then we shall indeed make a formidable team. Much like your 49ers."

She pulled him to his feet and encouraged him to drape his arm around her shoulders. He sagged against her and she almost staggered under his massive weight.

"We'll be okay, Sven. We love each other and that's a great place to start."

His knees buckled and he fell to the floor, bringing Thea down on top of him. His slow grin made her body melt against him. He slid a hand into her hair and brought her mouth down to meet his. His kiss branded her with the same intensity as the urgent press of his cock against her stomach.

"Then let us start right here."

Thea pulled away from him. "Some of us have work to do, you know."

He regarded her seriously even as his hand massaged her ass, grinding her sex against his shaft.

"Does this mean I get my job back?"

"As my lovely assistant?"

Sven frowned. "What does that mean? Do you expect me to sit by your desk, naked and chained, ready to service you whenever you require it?"

Thea sighed as the provocative image stirred every feminine molecule in her body. She kissed his luscious mouth and then his nose.

"Okay, you're hired."

Also by Kate Pearce

Antonia's Bargain
Eden's Pleasure
Planet Mail

About the Author

ଛ

Kate Pearce was born and bred in England. She spent most of her childhood being told that having a vivid imagination would never get her anywhere. After graduating from college with an honors degree in history, she ended up working in finance and spent even more time developing her deep innner life.

After relocating with her husband and family to Northern California in 1998, Kate fulfilled her dream and finally sat down to write her first novel. She writes in a variety of romance genres, although the Regency period is definitely her favorite.

Kate welcomes comments from readers. You can find her website and email address on her author bio page at www.ellorascave.com.

Tell Us What You Think

We appreciate hearing reader opinions about our books. You can email us at Comments@EllorasCave.com.

Why an electronic book?

We live in the Information Age—an exciting time in the history of human civilization, in which technology rules supreme and continues to progress in leaps and bounds every minute of every day. For a multitude of reasons, more and more avid literary fans are opting to purchase e-books instead of paper books. The question from those not yet initiated into the world of electronic reading is simply: *Why?*

1. *Price.* An electronic title at Ellora's Cave Publishing and Cerridwen Press runs anywhere from 40% to 75% less than the cover price of the exact same title in paperback format. Why? Basic mathematics and cost. It is less expensive to publish an e-book (no paper and printing, no warehousing and shipping) than it is to publish a paperback, so the savings are passed along to the consumer.

2. *Space.* Running out of room in your house for your books? That is one worry you will never have with electronic books. For a low one-time cost, you can purchase a handheld device specifically designed for e-reading. Many e-readers have large, convenient screens for viewing. Better yet, hundreds of titles can be stored within your new library—on a single microchip. There are a variety of e-readers from different manufacturers. You can also read e-books on your PC or laptop computer. (Please note that Ellora's Cave does not endorse any specific brands.

You can check our websites at www.ellorascave.com or www.cerridwenpress.com for information we make available to new consumers.)

3. *Mobility.* Because your new e-library consists of only a microchip within a small, easily transportable e-reader, your entire cache of books can be taken with you wherever you go.

4. ***Personal Viewing Preferences.*** Are the words you are currently reading too small? Too large? Too… ANNOYING? Paperback books cannot be modified according to personal preferences, but e-books can.

5. ***Instant Gratification.*** Is it the middle of the night and all the bookstores near you are closed? Are you tired of waiting days, sometimes weeks, for bookstores to ship the novels you bought? Ellora's Cave Publishing sells instantaneous downloads twenty-four hours a day, seven days a week, every day of the year. Our webstore is never closed. Our e-book delivery system is 100% automated, meaning your order is filled as soon as you pay for it.

Those are a few of the top reasons why electronic books are replacing paperbacks for many avid readers.

As always, Ellora's Cave and Cerridwen Press welcome your questions and comments. We invite you to email us at Comments@ellorascave.com or write to us directly at Ellora's Cave Publishing Inc., 1056 Home Avenue, Akron, OH 44310-3502.

COMING TO A BOOKSTORE NEAR YOU!

ELLORA'S CAVE

Bestselling Authors Tour

erridwen, the Celtic Goddess of wisdom, was the muse who brought inspiration to storytellers and those in the creative arts. Cerridwen Press encompasses the best and most innovative stories in all genres of today's fiction. Visit our site and discover the newest titles by talented authors who still get inspired - much like the ancient storytellers did, once upon a time.